The Living End
Frank Kane

Black Gat Books • Eureka California

THE LIVING END

Published by Black Gat Books
A division of Stark House Press
1315 H Street
Eureka, CA 95501, USA
griffinskye3@sbcglobal.net
www.starkhousepress.com

ISBN-13: 978-1-944520-84-7

Book design by Mark Shepard, shepgraphics.com
Cover art by Victor Kalin from the 1957 edition of
The Living End.
Proofreading by Bill Kelly

First Stark House Press/Black Gat Edition:
October 2019

1

Broadway between 49th and 50th Streets is Main Street of Tin Pan Alley, its Town Hall a nondescript stone building called the Brill, which houses on its ground floor Jack Dempsey's Restaurant and the Turf. Next to the building's main entrance are the doors to an oversized ballroom which once housed the lovelies of NTG's Paradise Restaurant. Outside on the sidewalk at all hours of the day and night musicians, song pluggers, and contact men stand clotted in little groups, blocking the pedestrians' progress with their instruments, filling the air with their conversation.

Eddie Marlon threaded his way through them, entered the dimness of the Brill lobby. Even in here the groups stretched the full length of the lobby, their heads inclined, muttering to each other in low, confidential tones. Eddie headed for the bank of elevators at the rear, checked the tenant register on the wall for Devine Music, pushed into the half-empty cage.

As the elevator moved upward to the fourth floor, Eddie Marlon drank in the atmosphere of the Brill. This was where he wanted to be, this was where he was headed.

He was thin and undersized, a fact that the carefully tailored blue suit and built-up shoulders failed to conceal. He wore no hat; a mass of thick, black hair rolled back in oily waves from his hairline. He wore his hair in a three-quarter part, which revealed the startling whiteness of his scalp. His thin lips were wreathed in a perpetual smile, but no trace of it showed in the eyes that squinted on either side of the high bridge of an enormous nose.

Under his arm he carried a large manila envelope. As the doors of the elevator opened, he unconsciously patted the envelope. Then he took a deep breath, stepped out into the fourth floor corridor.

Devine Music, Inc. was in 496, with three other music companies' names also stenciled on the door. He turned the knob, walked into an unlighted office that appeared to be no more than a storage space for old unsold sheet music which rose in stacks from the floor to the ceiling. Beyond there was a small inner office.

A man was sitting at the desk in the inner office, a sweat-stained fedora pushed to the back of his head. He looked up incuriously as Eddie Marlon walked in.

"I'm looking for Joseph Devine," Marlon told him.

The character behind the desk pulled a toothpick from between his lips, studied the macerated end. "Me," he conceded.

In addition to the desk the office's furnishings consisted of a battered spinet which bore service stripes made by cigarettes that had been left to burn unnoticed, a portable record player, and an open bookcase full of dusty books. A window that showed no signs of recent acquaintance with water looked out onto the airshaft.

"My name's Marlon." The thin kid looked around the office, tried to mask his disappointment with the ever-present smile. "I got a letter from you." He dug into his breast pocket. "About my song." He reached across the desk, handed the man a piece of note paper.

Devine took the letter, glanced at it. He flipped the paper back on the desk, looked up, and studied the other man. "How old are you, kid?"

Marlon shrugged. "Twenty-three."

The man in the chair rubbed the tips of his fingers

over the bristles that glinted along his jaw line. "You working? You got a job?"

"Yeah. But just filling in. I want to be a full-time song writer."

Devine flipped the chewed toothpick at the wastebasket, replaced it with a fresh one. "You got a copy of your song with you?"

Marlon nodded, opened the manila envelope, pulled out some sheets with rules and ink blots on them. "I only play the piano with one finger." He grinned. "But I figure if it's good enough for Irving Berlin, it's good enough for Eddie Marlon."

"Let's hear."

The piano was out of tune. Marlon made two false starts before he finally limped through the chorus. The song was reminiscent of half a dozen others that were currently popular. When he had finished, he looked anxiously at the man behind the desk. "What do you think?"

Devine shrugged. "What difference what I think? It's the public got to make or break a song." He pulled himself out of his chair, walked over to where an old water cooler stood against the wall, humming to itself. "You got the price of a demo?"

"A what?"

The man at the cooler filled a paper cup with water, sipped at it. "A demo. We got to have one so they can hear how it sounds."

"A record, you mean?"

Devine drained the cup, crushed it into a ball, tossed it at the wastebasket. "What else?" He walked back to the desk. "We get a good side on it, we take it to a big recording outfit, they like it, we're in."

Marlon shook his head. "I thought you were interested in publishing it. I thought—"

"So I publish it." He nodded his head toward the outer room where the baled sheet music reached to the ceiling. "I publish a lot of songs. Without it gets a play, they end up out there."

"But I thought that was what the publisher did. Get behind it and get it recorded."

"You kiddin'? You know what it costs to find out if you got a hit? About twenty-five grand." He pulled the toothpick from between his teeth, pointed at the sheet on the piano. "Maybe you got another 'Stardust' there, maybe it's just another dog." He replaced the toothpick, chewed on it. "Only way we get to know is get it on a platter and get one of the big boys to get behind it."

"Why should it cost so much?"

The music publisher grinned patronizingly. "The payola, boy, the old payola. You think maybe Brett Lyons is going to have his outfit play your song just because he likes your looks? You could look like Dracula and act like Frankenstein and he'll play hell out of it. If."

The boy at the piano picked up his music, shoved it back into the manila envelope. "But you said in your letter you'd consider publishing it. If you knew that—"

Devine shrugged. "So I'm considering it. But I'm also telling you we'd both be wasting our time."

"What chance do you think the song has?"

"Who knows?"

"I was just thinking that maybe if you have faith in it—"

"I'd pick up the hot?" Devine shook his head. "Hell, the way things are right now, I couldn't pick up the hot on a platter of flapjacks let alone a demo on a song written by somebody nobody ever heard of."

"Well, if that's the way it is."

"That's the way it is, kid. Believe me, you and me, we're in the wrong end of this business."

Marlon nodded. "Sounds like it."

"There's plenty of moolah in it, kid, plenty. But not at this end." Devine dropped back into his chair, tilted it back against the wall, laced his fingers at the nape of his neck. "You want to make some real loot, you get on the other end. Where they got to come to you to get their stuff played. Then you make them come, and often."

Marlon stood up dispiritedly. "Yeah, but how do you get to be a band leader if you can't even play 'Dixie' on a harmonica?"

"They sure got it made, those boys." Devine recognized the signs of disappointment and defeat on the thin boy's face. "What are you going to do now?"

Marlon shrugged. "I guess it would be a waste of time trying to sell this to one of the big publishers?"

Devine nodded. "Most of them got their own stable. They don't ever take a flyer on an unknown. Unless, like I said, you got a demo that really sells them."

"Confidentially, what do you think of this one?"

The man behind the desk pursed his lips. "It don't hit me," he admitted.

Marlon sighed. "I figured that."

"Even if it did, I still say you'd need a demo to crack a big outfit. They just don't waste time listening unless it's on a platter, and even then they pick up that arm before it's halfway through the chorus most of the time. They just ain't lookin'."

"Well, I guess it's back to the salt mines."

"What kind of job you got, kid?"

Marlon screwed his face into a grimace. "Shipping clerk." He looked around the unappetizing office. "Hate it like hell. This is the business I always wanted to be in."

"Say, I might know of a job if you're interested."

"What kind of a job?"

"Lousy hours."

"Doing what?"

Devine let the front legs of his chair hit the floor. "You ever hear Marty Allen on WTLO?"

Marlon nodded. "He's got one of those wake-up programs. Spins records, tells a few jokes. That the guy?"

"Yeah. I hear he's looking for a guy to help him."

"You mean talk over the radio and—"

Devine shook his head. "He's a pushover, but not that much of a pushover. He wants somebody to get in a couple of hours before he does and set up the show for the day. Pick the records, get everything set."

"A couple of hours before he does? What time is that?"

The music publisher grinned at him. "He goes on the air at six. You'd probably have to be there at four."

Marlon grimaced. "At four? That's the middle of the night."

"You said you were sick of being a shipping clerk." Devine shrugged. "I thought you'd like a change."

"At four o'clock in the morning?" The thin kid groaned. "It'd be better if I stayed up all night."

"You could do that, too. In a spot like that maybe you could even put the arm on contact men so it wouldn't cost you a dime. They all got swindle sheets, they pick up the hot."

"You think so?" The ready smile broadened, then it drained away. "Allen would probably chew me out for moving in on his racket."

Devine pursed his lips, considered that. "He don't have to know."

"You think the contact men are going to stand still to pick up the checks for two people for that one mangy little radio program?"

"You don't have to worry about that. Allen does it strictly for no."

"For no?"

"No dough. One hundred per cent no take."

"Must be because nobody offered," Marlon said gloomily. "After all what good's it do anybody to get their songs played before anybody's awake?"

"Let them worry about that. You make it sound like it's real important. Don't forget, like you said four a.m. is the middle of the night to most people. But not to these characters. Most of them are just driving home or sitting in some gin mill getting a nightcap. You think it occurs to them ordinary people are still in the pad?"

"Well, anyway, it'd be better than being a shipping clerk."

"Want I should call him?"

"Yeah."

Devine uncurled from his chair. "You got a dime?" He waited while the boy fumbled through his pockets, came up with a coin. "Pay phone," he explained, nodding to the tarnished instrument on the wall.

2

The date was set for eleven o'clock the next day in Murphy's, a little hole in the wall stuck between a novelty shop and a camera store on Madison Avenue in the Fifties. Convenient to the Republic Broadcasting Building, it got a big play day and night from the artists and announcers on the network.

Eddie Marlon was on his second cup of coffee and his third fingernail when Marty Allen walked in. He was heavy-set, looked good-natured. His hair had begun to recede and as the result of his refusal to wear a hat in any kind of weather, his forehead was freckled. He was wearing a nubby tweed jacket and contrasting slacks, a sport shirt open at the collar. He leaned across the counter, talked to the counterman, who pointed to the booth where Eddie Marlon sat.

He walked down to Marlon's booth, slid in opposite him. "Hope I didn't keep you waiting, kid. We're getting a new sponsor on the show and I had to meet the ad man on the account."

Marlon grinned. "Don't worry about it." He studied the big man opposite him, decided he was probably a pretty good guy, but not too much on the brains side. "I guess now you can go on home and go back to bed."

Allen motioned to a waitress. "You kidding? My day's just beginning." He waved aside the coffee-stained menu. "Just bring me some coffee, Mary. I've got an early lunch date." When the waitress had shuffled back toward the kitchen, he turned back to the skinny kid opposite him. "I've got to spend a lot of time with the boys from the ad agencies. They're the kids that pay the bills, you know."

"You mean you've got to sell advertising, too?"

Allen grinned. "It's not quite that bad—yet. No, I don't hustle the commercials, I just peddle them. We've got advertising salesmen to take care of that end. But it doesn't hurt to know the boys and to get along with them."

The waitress set a cup of coffee in front of him, raised her eyebrows at Marlon. He shook his head. "I've had enough." She scratched some figures on a slip of paper, dropped it on the table, and retreated in the direction of the kitchen.

"You sound like you have your hands full," Eddie

Marlon said.

"That's only half of it, kid. There's a lot of civic work I get sucked in on. They want name performers for rallies and things and I'm their boy." He sipped at his coffee, burned his tongue, growled under his breath. "Pays off, though. Most of the guys working on the committee are business men, people who know the value of advertising. We get a lot of business that way, too."

"Devine told me you could use an assistant."

The disc jockey sipped cautiously at his coffee, managed to swallow some without scalding his mouth. "He tell you the hours?"

Marlon nodded.

"You still want it?"

"Yeah. I'm a song writer. He tell you that?"

Allen leaned back, shook his head. "He just said you needed a job."

"Well, maybe I should have said I want to be a song writer. In the meantime I've got to eat."

"Had anything published?"

Marlon shook his head ruefully. "I only wrote one. I guess it's no world-beater. But I'm going to stick at it."

"Good for you. This job might be helpful. Being around music and listening to it day after day, you might pick up the formula." He checked his watch, winced. "I've got to get going if I'm going to make that date on time. Suppose you meet me at the station in the morning at four. I'll show you how I go about arranging the day's show and you can make up your mind if the job's for you."

"Devine didn't mention any salary."

The disc jockey pursed his lips. "I think I can get you fifty. How's that?"

"It's more than I'm getting," Marlon said.

"All right, then. I'll expect you at four. It's Studio 107B. On the fifth floor of Republic. You know where the side entrance to the building is?"

The thin boy shook his head.

"It's on the 47th Street side. You just rap on the door, tell the watchman you're meeting me. I'll leave word to okay you through."

"I'll be there, Mr. Allen."

"Marty, kid. Mr. Allen's my father." He winked, wiped at his mouth with a paper napkin, got up and hustled toward the door. He stopped at the cashier's cage, dropped a bill, and waved.

Eddie Marlon watched while the man's broad back disappeared through the doorway, melted into the thin stream of pedestrians on the avenue. He sat back, took stock, decided that what Marty Allen could use was a smart young boy. A smart young boy named Eddie Marlon, for example.

Eddie Marlon hadn't always been his name, but the fierce ambition had always been part of him. Even as Eddie Bronowski, an undersized little Polish kid in Brooklyn, he had been determined to carve himself a spot in the world outside.

His first attempt to pull himself out of his rut was a brief sortie into the Golden Gloves. He won his first fight by default, failed to duck a haymaker in the first round of his second fight and decided the ring was not for him.

Then he came across the legend of Billy Rose—the stenographer who carefully dissected popular songs, reassembled a reasonable facsimile and had a hit in "Barney Google." Eddie Marlon studied the pictures of Billy Rose, decided that this might very well be his forte. If a pint-sized stenographer could make the grade to the easy pickings of song writing, why couldn't a similarly pint-sized Eddie Marlon?

He had haunted the library studying the lyrics of songs that had left a mark on the public. He had devised what he considered to be a foolproof system for constructing a hit by lifting a few bars here, a few bars there and welding them into a whole that was reminiscent of the best of each of the pirated numbers.

Tirelessly he had sent it from publisher to publisher, only to have it returned in its original envelope unopened. He had just about exhausted the list of publishers in the telephone classified section when he discovered a magazine named *Current Hits* on the newsstand. After running through it, he realized that here was where he'd find the publisher who would bring his song to the attention of the public. Page after page of classified advertisements invited would-be song writers to submit their songs for "appraisal, criticism and collaboration" with an eye toward having them published,

One ad, in particular, had been intriguing. It read:

Song Writers! An established publisher is looking for your songs, object publication. We have published hundreds, many by unknowns, that are now being sung over the radio and played on juke boxes. Let us see a sample of your work. Devine Music Co., Brill Building, New York.

When the manuscript went out the next morning Eddie Bronowski disappeared and in his place was Eddie Marlon, song writer. An impatient Eddie Marlon who rushed home from work every night looking for the letter from the Devine Music Co. that would change his whole life.

It finally arrived a week after the manuscript had gone out. A short businesslike note from Joseph Devine, President of Devine Music Co., informing Mr. Eddie Marlon that he would be interested in discussing with him personally the possibilities of Devine Music publishing his song. Would he drop around to the office the first of the following week?

At that moment Eddie Marlon shucked everything that had been Eddie Bronowski—the dingy flat on East 7th Street, the mother who still labored painfully to overcome a heavy Polish accent, the job that had been slowly grinding him to a pulp.

Over the tearful protests of his mother, he had gathered his few belongings, a copy of his precious song, and had turned his back on the past. Eddie Marlon would need none of the things that had been Eddie Bronowski. He was on his way.

New York City is a different place at four in the morning. The roar of traffic has dwindled to a hum. The streets are deserted, a light mist seems to gather around the street lamps, diffusing their light to a soft blurry yellow. The empty sidewalks stretch for what seems miles, with only an occasional store front spilling a pool of light onto the sidewalk.

Eddie Marlon got off the Sixth Avenue subway at Rockefeller Center, walked along 49th Street. An occasional cab barreled west from an east-side call, passing the time until it could head for the garage. The RCA Building loomed over him, tall, dark, and deserted, the Plaza itself lay wrapped in shadow, resting from a busy day of hurrying feet, grinding tires, restless activity.

At Fifth a sudden gust of wind caused him to shudder and turn his collar up around his neck. The wind caught a half sheet of a morning tabloid and sent it skirling up the avenue to come to rest on the flight of steps leading to the cathedral.

He quickened his pace, headed for Murphy's. He just had time for a hot cup of coffee before he met Allen. As he walked, head sunk into his collar, he thought if it was this bad the first day, how much worse it would get as the days went by. Suddenly, in retrospect, being a shipping clerk began to have some merits.

He slid onto a stool in Murphy's, glanced up at the clock over the counter. So he'd be a few minutes late! Without the coffee he couldn't make it at all.

A bored counterman stood at the far end of the counter, drying cups with a damp rag, listening with half an ear to the woes of a faded and blowzy blonde who alternately sipped at her cold coffee and swabbed at her nose with a gray-white handkerchief.

"Let's have a coffee, mac," Marlon called.

The counterman nodded, took his time about finishing the cup. He took a last puff on his cigarette, balanced it on an overturned cup, shuffled to the coffee urn. He drew a steaming cup of coffee, slid it in front of the thin kid. "Danish?"

"Nothing. Just coffee." Marlon dug a quarter from his jacket pocket, slid it across the counter.

The blonde looked the kid over appreciatively, perked up. She dabbed her damp nose dry, tried a smile for effect. It didn't make it. When she saw Marlon was paying no attention, she returned to muttering to her coffee.

Eddie dug a cigarette from his jacket pocket, hung it in the corner of his mouth. He lighted it, took a deep breath, exhaled twin streams from his nostrils. Then, with a glance at the clock, he got the scalding coffee inside him.

The watchman at the side door of Republic was expecting him. He opened the door, carefully locked it after Eddie was in, and led the way to a freight elevator in the rear.

The cage whined and groaned its way to a jarring stop at the fifth floor.

"Mr. Allen's studio is the fourth one on your left. He's expecting you."

Marlon nodded his thanks, walked down the empty corridor, his heels echoing hollowly against the concrete floors.

The door to Studio 107B was open. Marty Allen sat at an unvarnished desk in the center of the room. At his left elbow was a pile of recordings, in front of him a sheaf of paper and a drinking glass filled with freshly sharpened pencils.

He looked up as Eddie Marlon walked in. "Hello, kid. I thought maybe you got lost." He picked up a platter, examined the titles on both sides. Then, frowning, he scribbled a notation on the paper in front of him. "Pull up a chair and I'll explain what goes."

He leaned back in the big armchair, watched while Eddie pulled a straight-backed wooden chair to the opposite side of the desk.

"Smoke?" The disc jockey indicated a pack of cigarettes on the corner of his desk. Marlon reached over, took one, settled into his chair. "Ready?"

The thin kid nodded. "I guess this might sound like a stupid question, but how come it takes two hours every day to line up the records? I mean why not just pick 'em out and spin them?"

"That's not too stupid. The reason we do it this way is to try to keep our audience. The other way, we might lose half of them."

"Why?"

"Well, for one thing, we'd probably be playing some sides a lot more than others. That could get boring. You can't give them all schmaltz any more than you can give them all boogie. You've got to mix it up, keep everybody happy." He stuck a cigarette in the corner of his mouth where it waggled when he talked. "Make sense?"

Marlon considered it, nodded. "Plenty."

"Another thing, you've got to be careful in switching from one type to another. You get them dreamy with schmaltz and then you blast them with boogie and you're liable to send them running screaming. Don't forget, the people listening to us are guys getting ready to go to work, they're women who are shuffling around half asleep getting the kids off to school. You've got to ease them into a change of mood." He picked up a couple of records. "He's an example of where we're using three sides to get from 'Blue Skies' to 'Rampart Street Blues.' That way we don't jolt them."

Marlon studied the big man with increased respect. "It don't show, all that framework, I mean. You sit and listen to the show, you figure there's a guy sitting at a desk, just reaching into his files playing records."

"That way, chances are all you'd be playing would be the real boffs. That would gyp you out of half the fun of this job."

"What's that?"

"The sleepers. Lots of times a record's going so hot most of the dee-jays never flip it. Sometimes the jump side's a real sleeper and the first guy to find it out's got himself a first." He scribbled a title on his sheet. "I've come up with a lot of them. Used to be that a recording company would back a sure thing with a dog. But they can't do that now that the jukes can play either side."

Marlon looked around. "Mind if I explore?"

"Go ahead. I'll finish this up, then we can check the commercials."

The thin kid got up, walked over to the large glass window that separated the engineer and the director from the studio. Inside, he could see three large turntables, an imposing looking panel board, and ceiling-high electrical contraptions.

"The records get played in the booth?" he asked.

Allen looked up, nodded. "I cue them in from here." He nodded to the desk. "They set my mike up on the desk and I do the intros and the sell right here."

"What do you do while the record's playing?" Marlon walked back to the desk, tapped off a thin collar of ash from the end of his cigarette.

"Read through the next commercial, make sure I've got it pat. Maybe even jack it up. If it's a rainy day, I make reference to it in my aspirin commercial. It gives the program a sort of an up-to-the-minute taste."

Marlon grinned ruefully. "I guess I underrated you guys. From where I sat it was the easiest racket in the world. Now I'm not so sure."

The man behind the desk pointed his pencil at him. "You have to keep remembering one thing, kid. You're in here to entertain, sure. But the real reason you're in here is to sell. When you forget that, kid, you're out. They all love you, sure, but only when you're selling their stuff like crazy. The day that buy drops off, you drop dead."

"It figures," Eddie said. "Only I never looked at it that way."

Allen bent his head over his list again, frowned in concentration as he changed the listing of the titles he had written on the sheet. "Just poke around today and get the feel of the place. You can start learning this end of it in the next couple of days."

"How about new records? How do you keep up on that?"

The frown on Allen's face was replaced with a grin. "That's the easiest part of this. You don't have to do a thing. The recording companies all have contact men. They're usually lined up in the hall waiting for me when I get off." He tossed the pencil down, looked up at Marlon from under half-lowered lids. "Maybe we ought to talk a little bit about that, kid." He took a last drag from his cigarette, crushed it out. "Sit down."

Marlon dropped into the chair. "Talk about what?"

"Contact men." Allen leaned back, touched the tips of his fingers across his stomach. "You'll be in a position where some of them are going to be romancing you."

"To schedule their records?" He decided to play it straight.

Allen nodded. "Every one of them. Some of them are even going to suggest they could make it worth your while." He shrugged. "It's been done. But we don't play that way." He stared unblinkingly at Marlon. "Am I coming in, kid?"

"Real strong, Marty."

"That's the way I want it, kid. That's the way it's got to be."

3

In spite of early misgivings, Eddie Marlon found himself falling very comfortably into the pattern of life demanded by his new job. Now, instead of rising at seven and rushing to a job he hated, he found himself getting up at almost the time he used to get home.

He found almost all of his relaxation in the Broadway area—on the cuff—leaving when the clubs closed to head for Studio 107B.

Once there, he would lay out a suggested list of selections for Marty Allen, who would check it with an experienced eye, nod his approval. Once in a while he would underline a title with his thumb nail.

"Instead of using Carla Hoff's cutting, use Betty Saint's. She did the original version. The Hoff one's just a cover by a big company."

"But Hoff's a bigger name, Marty," Eddie would argue.

"Sure, but the other kid's on her way up. And the way to give her a lift is to play her version. It was hers in the first place."

Eddie Marlon never argued with Allen. He made it a point never to make a positive guarantee to a pusher that he could schedule their sides. He agreed to do his best, and that's the way it had to stand. Nevertheless, he occasionally took a chance on slipping through one he'd agreed to plug—for a consideration. Despite Marty Allen's bovinely good-natured appearance, Marlon knew he was sharp as a tack and a hard man to fool, so he kept the special sides to a minimum.

Eddie Marlon had been on the job almost nine months when he first met Jo Leary. A contact man from Rhythm Records, Mike Shannon, had been selling her heavily for days and Eddie finally agreed to drop by the Shamrock Club with him to catch her number. She had waxed two sides for Rhythm, and Shannon was charged with the job of getting her record promotion and publicity. To date he hadn't been able to get himself arrested as far as Marty Allen's program was concerned and he was getting ready to turn the heavy guns on Eddie.

The Shamrock was a chromium-plated nightery with a multicolored canopy that extended to the curb. As Eddie's cab pulled up to the curb, a seven-foot giant in the full regalia of an admiral made a production of opening the door for him.

Eddie stepped out, waited while Mike Shannon pushed a bill through the window to the cabby. Then he followed the plugger across the sidewalk to where the doorman stood holding the plate-glass doors open.

Inside, the Shamrock was dim, intimate. Shannon tossed his hat to the hat-check girl. He dropped a bill on the tray, picked up a pack of Chesterfields. "How's your love life, honey?" he greeted the girl.

"Empty without you, doll." The hat-check girl didn't pause in the act of adding another layer of paint to her already flaming lips. "You haven't been true to me. Where you been?" She studied her handiwork in a small pocket mirror.

"Business, baby."

"Monkey business," she agreed. "You in to see the Bombshell?"

Shannon nodded. "How's she been doing?"

"Killing them." Her eyes jumped from Shannon to Eddie Marlon. "We've had the ropes up every night for the past week. She's hotter than a fifty-cent pistol."

A two-hundred-pound fashion plate in a midnight blue tuxedo came up to greet them as they walked into the dining-room beyond. The headwaiter wore a red carnation in his lapel, a lazy smile was pasted on his lips. His hair was thick and white; his eyes tired and dull. "Good evening, Mr. Shannon. Table or bar?"

"Table, Kurt." He nodded to Eddie Marlon. "This is Ed Marlon of the Marty Allen show. Ever catch it?"

The white-haired man nodded. "I always read awhile

after I get home. Turn the radio to his show." He looked the thin man over with a semblance of interest. "You do a good job. Like the show, very much." He turned back to Shannon. "I have a very nice table for you, Mr. Shannon."

The man in the blue tuxedo snapped his fingers and fussily adjusted his cuffs while he waited for a captain to scurry over. He pulled a menu from under the captain's arm and motioned for Shannon and his guest to follow him. He led the way down three red-carpeted steps and around past the tables that skirted the dance floor. The one he selected faced the bandstand, had an unobstructed view of the floor.

"Will this be all right?" Kurt asked solicitously.

Shannon looked around and nodded. He passed a folded bill to the headwaiter. "Fine, Kurt. What time does Jo go on?"

"The floor show will be starting any moment now. Can I have the waiter bring you a drink, sir?"

The plugger slid into a chair, nodded. "I'll have Forester on the rocks. How about you, Eddie?"

"Same."

They sat and talked desultorily until the waiter brought their drinks, then they drank silently. It was obvious that Shannon had given up his hard sell and was counting on the girl to soften Marlon up.

Finally the band blared an introductory chord and the house lights dimmed. A yellow spot probed through the semidarkness, picked up the emcee as he pranced out onto the floor. He was tall and thin, had unbelievably broad shoulders and walked with a peculiarly mincing step.

Even from where Eddie sat, the emcee's teeth looked too white and too even to be real. He fluttered through a couple of off-color jokes that brought a faint ripple of applause and sang two nasal choruses of a number never destined to become popular by his rendition. Then he raised his hands to cut off the almost nonexistent applause to introduce "the rest of our show."

He gave way to a line of girls in spangled brassieres and satin pants. They scampered around the dance floor, bare legs flashing, bare stomachs undulating. When their number was finally finished, they ran off the floor and the house lights dimmed.

The sporadic applause died away and an expectant hush seemed to fall over the room. From somewhere, the lisping voice of the master of ceremonies filled the room. "And now, the star of our show—Miss Jo Leary, Miss Snow Top herself—the one you've been waiting for!"

When the lights went up, a piano had been wheeled to the center of the floor. A tall, voluptuously built platinum blonde stood next to it. Her hair was blue white, complemented by the deep tan of her face and bare shoulders. She wore a daringly décolleté white satin gown that clung to her generous curves, seemed to be having trouble restraining full, thrusting breasts. A small waist accented the full hips, the long shapely legs concealed by the fullness of the skirt. Her mouth was a vivid, moist crimson slash in the cocoa color of her face; her eyes were startlingly blue.

The entire room seemed to release its breath in a slow sigh as she started to sway in rhythm with the torch song the band began to play.

Marlon looked from the floor to the man opposite him, pursed his lips in a soundless whistle. The plugger grinned back. "Wait'll you hear her."

The blonde's voice was intimate, sultry. The lyrics of her song were blue and off color, but she managed an expression of untroubled innocence despite the burst of laughter some of the lines drew. At the end of the number, she grinned at the explosion of applause and the scattered wolf calls, and permitted herself to be coaxed into an encore.

She held up her hand. "As long as you're all so nice," she breathed, rather than talked, "I'd like to sing for you my latest recorded number just released by Rhythm Records." She looked in their direction. "And I'd like to dedicate it to Mr. Eddie Marlon." She held the palm of her hand to her mouth, blew a kiss.

Marlon looked over to where Shannon sat smirking. "What's that all about?"

Shannon shrugged. "She's just the grateful type. I told her you were a fan of hers and so she was showing her appreciation." He dumped a Chesterfield from the pack, held it out to Eddie. "You'd be surprised what a grateful girl she can be."

Marlon took a cigarette, stared thoughtfully at the circle of light in the center of the floor that framed the swaying figure of the blonde. He could feel the perspiration on his forehead and upper lip.

Jo Leary was followed by an adagio team of questionable agility. They were almost through their number when a uniformed pageboy came up to Shannon's table.

"Mr. Shannon?" The plugger acknowledged the question with a nod. "Miss Leary would like to see you and your friend in her dressing-room."

"Like to meet her, Eddie?" Shannon asked.

The thin man ran the flat of his palm against the hair over his ear, smoothed it back. "Why not?"

They followed the pageboy around the back of the room to a door leading backstage. The glitter and tinsel of the dining-room had no counterpart backstage at the Shamrock. Backstage consisted of a dingy, uncarpeted corridor lined on both sides with doors. It smelled exotically of one part perfume to three parts perspiration.

Jo Leary's dressing-room door was identifiable by a peeling gilt star. The pageboy rapped at the door, waited expectantly.

"Come in," a sultry, disturbing voice invited.

She was sitting on a straight-backed chair in front of a make-up table. She had exchanged the white, tightfitting dress for a light blue dressing-gown that made it quite obvious that her assets were as liquid as those of the First National City Bank.

She grinned at the wide-eyed, slack-lipped stare of the pageboy, winked at him. "You remember what I said, Mickey. You come back when you're a big boy. You hear?"

The pageboy retreated in confusion, the blonde turned her attention on Eddie Marlon. If she was disappointed in his size, there was no evidence of it in the blue eyes or the welcoming smile.

"Shannon's been telling me all about you," she told him throatily. "I'm glad you could come by to say hello." From up close her eyes were startlingly blue; the corners crinkled when she smiled. She got up from the chair, motioned him to it, perched on the edge of her dressing-table. "How'd you like the number?"

"Has plenty of sock. The way you do it."

She pouted prettily. "Then how come you never play it on your program? I listen to you every morning and—"

"It's Marty Allen you hear, honey," Shannon corrected her hastily. "Eddie here's the boy behind the scenes. He sets up what Allen plays and says."

"All the more reason," she batted long eyelashes at Eddie. "It would mean so much to me if you'd get behind my record, and—"

"I'd like to, honey." Eddie grinned weakly. "But it's like Shannon says. It's the Marty Allen Show, not the Eddie Marlon Show. I had you skedded, but Marty thinks it's too early in the morning to belt them with a number like that."

"You could use your influence." She accepted a cigarette from Shannon, screwed it into a long holder, put the holder between her teeth, and waited for a light. Shannon provided it. "It would mean so much to me." She let the smoke dribble from between parted lips. "So very much."

"It could make the platter, Eddie. We've already got an okay from the juke-box boys on placing it. If we get any kind of a play on the air and the jukes get behind it, we're in. That's why we need a break from you so badly."

"As simple as that, eh?"

Shannon shrugged. "I'm not trying to kid you. Plugging, promotion, publicity and plenty of play will make any side. We'll take care of the plugging and the publicity and the promotion. If you'll take care of the repetition."

Marlon couldn't take his eyes off the blonde. "What's in it for me?"

The blonde returned his stare from under half-closed, colored lids. "The record's already cut up in more pieces than Carnera. But I'll make it up to you. In other ways."

4

The Spotlight Residence Club was an old-fashioned hotel located between Broadway and Sixth in the dingy West Forties. It had a faded awning that showed signs of having waged a losing battle with time and strong winds. Nobody had bothered to patch the gaping rips that flapped noisily in the breeze. The building's façade was dirty and neglected-looking.

The dim little lobby had the requisite number of tired rubber plants, a few chairs obviously unsafe to sit on, and a general air of decay. The girl behind the newsstand counter perked up as Eddie Marlon walked in; she pushed a few stray wisps of blondined hair into place with the tips of her fingers and eyed him expectantly. The interest drained out as he walked past, headed for the shabby registration desk and the rheumy-eyed old man who presided over it.

The room clerk blew his nose noisily as Marlon approached.

"You got a Jo Leary living here?" the thin man wanted to know.

The old man stowed his handkerchief in his hip pocket. He glanced at the speckled face of the alarm clock on his desk, sucked on his teeth noisily. "Yeah, but she ain't up yet. Never sees anybody this early."

"She'll see me. Try her." Marlon dug into his pocket, brought out a bill, folded it suggestively.

The old man looked undecided, puffed out his lips. "She expecting you, mister?" The rheumy eyes caressed the folded bill.

"Try her."

"Ring the Leary girl's room, May," the old man called

to a faded middle-aged woman who presided over an old-fashioned switchboard. "Tell her Mr.—" He eyed the thin man questioningly.

"Marlon, Eddie Marlon."

"—Eddie Marlon is here to see her." He made no attempt to get his hand out of the way when Marlon shoved the bill across the counter at him.

The woman jabbed wearily at a key on the board. After a moment she pulled the plug. "Mad as a wet hen," she sniffed. "Always is if you call her this hour of the day." She looked at Marlon accusingly. "She sure wasn't expecting him."

"Okay for him to go up?" the old man cut her off.

The woman shrugged, went back to her magazine.

"Room 336," the clerk told Marlon, and after a moment was lost in rapt consideration of an operation he was performing on a molar with a dirty fingernail.

At the third floor, Eddie Marlon followed a threadbare rug that had once been red but now was a brownish pink with numerous breaks and worn spots where the backing showed through.

Jo Leary opened the door in response to his knock. She wore a clinging hostess gown that made it clear she wore nothing under it. Her blue-white hair, cascading down to her shoulders, was caught just behind her ears with a blue ribbon. Her eyes were still clouded with sleep.

"You sure don't waste any time taking a girl up on an invitation," she complained. She watched him walk past her, toss his hat at a chair.

"Nice place you got here."

She kicked the door shut. "It's a dump and you know it."

"Okay, so we're past the formalities." He pulled a bottle of vodka from under his arm, held it out. "Just thought you might have some tomato juice with nothing to do."

"Not tomato juice. Plenty of orange juice." She read the label on the bottle. "This is the stuff that's supposed to leave you breathless."

"Well, if that doesn't, maybe my news will." He walked over, dropped onto the couch. "Your disc is getting four successive plays on the Allen show this week. Special favor from me to you."

Her soft-looking lips peeled back from a perfect set of teeth. "Wonderful. You're a doll!"

"Yeah, ain't I? That all you got to tell me?"

"Not half." She walked over, bent over him, covered his mouth with hers. The front of her gown sagged open; she gave no sign of noticing it.

"That Smirnoff's got a lot to learn from you, baby. In the leaving breathless department, I mean." He reached for her to pull her down onto his lap, she eluded his grasp, danced toward the kitchen. She reappeared a few minutes later carrying a tray with some ice cubes, glasses, and a large pitcher of orange juice.

"Does Shannon know about the play?" she asked.

Marlon nodded, dropped three ice cubes into each of the glasses, washed them with vodka. Then he added the orange juice and stirred.

"How come this is your first disc? I think you're loaded with talent."

The blonde walked over to an armchair, dropped into it. She picked up a cigarette, screwed it into a holder, placed that in the corner of her mouth. "I never did any real pop stuff before. You caught my act at the Shamrock. That number I did was only an encore. The rest is special material."

"But that other stuff you do. That's real solid."

Jo lighted the cigarette, filled her lungs with smoke,

blew it at the ceiling. "Not for a recording. That's special stuff for people who're doing a little drinking and a lot of relaxing. They come there with the idea of having you entertain them so they listen to the lyrics and it gets to them. You put that on a deejay show and the guy who's driving to work, or the truckdriver, or the woman doing her housework—they haven't got time to listen to words and lyrics. You've got to give them something simple like June-moon-spoon."

Marlon sipped at his drink, approved. "I'm not too sure about that."

"I am." The blonde reached for her glass, set it down on the end table next to her chair. "I've been living with it. How many of Noel Coward's records get on the Hit Parade? Or any of those real cute guys? Unless you listen real close you miss the message and people who listen to deejays don't have the time to listen close. Give them Irving Berlin or Oscar Hammerstein. That they can dig without listening."

"Well, anyway, Marty promised to let me sked your side for the next four days." He lifted his glass. "Good luck."

She lifted hers. "Luck." She took a deep swallows wrinkled her nose.

"You like?"

She cocked her head, considered. "Yeah. But I'm afraid of it."

"Why?"

"Experience. Anything that tastes that good must be bad for you."

Marlon chuckled. "How can it be bad? It's got orange juice to build you up."

"And alcohol to tear you down."

"So the worst that can happen is you come out even."

She took another deep swallow from her glass, set it

down. "You know, Eddie, I appreciate the break you're getting me." She leaned back in the chair, her breasts jutting against the flimsy fabric of the gown. "How can I ever thank you?"

He patted the cushion alongside him. "I told you I'd do everything I could for you." He watched as she pulled herself out of the chair, walked toward him. The sway of her breasts traced designs on the shiny fabric of her robe. She dropped down beside him. "I intend to do a lot more," he said.

"You're sweet," the blonde said. He was aware of her nearness, of the pressure of her thigh against his, of the warm, musky smell of her. "I knew that on the night Mike Shannon brought you backstage." She swung her feet up on the couch, laid her head in his lap.

"How come I've never seen you before, baby? Haven't you worked in the East?"

"I haven't worked, period." She ran her fingers through his thick, black hair. "You remember Charley Droppi?"

Marlon wrinkled his forehead. "The mobster?"

She nodded. "They used to call him Three Fingers."

"I remember him. He got knocked off in California. About a year ago. That the guy?"

"Eight months to be exact." She ran the tips of her fingers down his jaw, caressed his chin. "I was living with Charley when they got him."

"Why?"

She shrugged. "They said he was holding out some Syndicate money in Vegas. They didn't give him a chance to explain, they—"

"I don't mean that. I mean why should a dish like you play house with a fat greaseball like him?"

She veiled her eyes with long-lashed lids. "You want

to hear the story of my life? It's not pretty." She swung her feet down to the floor, sat up, and reached for her drink. "But, you know something? If I had it all to do over again, I've got a sneaking hunch I'd do it exactly the same way."

"Why Droppi?"

"I was hoofing in Chicago at one of the big joints on the Near North Side, three or four years ago. All of us in the line were on the lookout for some of these characters that were supposed to light cigars with hundred-dollar bills. Jackie Miles was headlining the show this week and when he comes back after his number he mentions that Three Fingers Droppi is at ringside." She swirled her drink around in the glass. "I knew all about this character. He used thousand-dollar bills instead of centuries. So I decided to get next to him."

Marlon looked her over, grinned. "I'll bet he never knew what hit him!"

"I was a redhead that year. Charley was a pushover for redheads." She drained her glass, set it back on the coffee table. "First thing you know, Charley's got me out of the chorus and I'm taking voice lessons from a fag on the North Side. But this guy really knows his stuff and before I know what's happening Charley has me booked as a chantoosie in one of the spots he has an interest in. I'm going real good, real big, when he breaks the news to me one night that the Syndicate wants him to take over a new spot in Vegas."

Marlon did a refill job on the girl's glass. "So by-by career?"

The blonde nodded. "Not quite that sudden, but by-by career. Charley don't want to leave me in Chicago where a half a dozen other wolves are beginning to give me the eye; but on the other hand, with him the Big Shot in the Vegas operation, he don't want me working out there. So, he makes me the proposition that he'll take over on the bills and I can live like a lady."

"Tough break. Him getting it, I mean."

The blonde shrugged, held her glass aloft, took a deep swallow. "Not too tough. When Charley got it, some of the boys came to see me. They told me I wouldn't have to worry. Not about money, anyway."

"How's that?

She grinned at him. "You wouldn't be playing square for mama, would you, dad? You know the Syndicate owns the Shamrock. You got a pretty damn' good idea the Syndicate owns the juke-box concession. So, how come I get the top slot at the Shamrock and a big play on the jukes?"

Marlon considered it. "You're double lucky."

"Why double?"

"The boys get mad at your man for crossing them, but they don't get mad at you. They go out of their way to see you're taken care of."

"That add up to something?"

"I was wondering why a gun-smart guy like Charley Droppi would let them put him on the spot when he knew they were after him." He shrugged. "But that's none of my business."

She nodded. "That's right. That's none of your business." She looked over at the little clock on the table. "I've got an appointment with the hairdresser in an hour."

He slid his arm around her, pulled her against him. She buried her fingers in his hair, pulled his mouth against hers. Her lips were soft, eager.

After a moment he pulled away. "I think maybe you better cancel that appointment, baby."

"So do I." She found his mouth again with hers,

shuddered uncontrollably. Her nails dug into his shoulders, his back. He could feel her sharp little teeth gnawing at his lip. He picked her up, carried her across the floor.

5

The Jo Leary interlude lasted almost two weeks. Then, unaccountably, she stopped answering her telephone and was never in when Eddie Marlon dropped by. At first he was peeved, but after a while he philosophically accepted the fact that when he was no longer able to deliver the merchandise she was in the market to buy, she no longer felt constrained to pay. Once, weeks later, when he accidentally bumped into her in a restaurant, she was distantly cordial. Almost as if she couldn't quite remember his name. By then he was resigned to the fact that it hadn't been his own fatal charm that had brought her into his arms in the first place.

With almost a year as Marty Allen's assistant under his belt, Eddie Marlon was becoming a figure in the radio and music world. Marty still kept a tight rein on him, made him keep his contracts with the pluggers down to a reasonable minimum. On the other hand, he wasn't averse to the little guy making an occasional buck by giving a disc a ride for a few days.

"I don't mind a little larceny, kid," he drawled one day as he drew a black line through a record that had been showing up with monotonous regularity on the morning list. "It's just that we've got listeners to please. We turn this show over to the pluggers and we're going to be talking to ourselves."

Marlon never resented the big man. He did sometimes despise him as a square for not exploiting the opportunities he had with a program like this under him; but Allen was always consistent—he wasn't on the take himself, was happily married, and brushed off the Jo Leary kind of payola. So the kid couldn't logically hate him for holding a tight rein on him.

One night, months later, sitting with Mike Shannon, the plugger, in the Hawaiian Paradise, a little upholstered sewer on West 52nd Street, Marlon complained of the lost opportunities he had to bear.

"I'd like to have a crack at that show for just a year," he grunted. "I'd show you how to get the most out of it."

Shannon sat opposite him, making tangential circles with the bottom of his glass on the table top. "Good thing you're not. It's tough enough on us guys now. My office is screaming over the swindle I turn in as it is." He looked toward the dance floor, peered through the clouds of stagnant smoke that hovered over them. "Ever see this Rose LaRue? She does a strip makes Margie Hart look like a schoolmarm."

On the postage-stamp-sized dance floor a motley group of musicians were straggling out to take their places on gilt chairs clustered on a small raised platform. As they slumped into their chairs, each one picked up his instrument and started to warm up, creating a cacophony.

"Don't tell me this one's got a platter, too?" Marlon asked and grinned.

Shannon shook his head. "Wish she had. This is real stuff." He pulled his eyes away from the floor. "Ever see the Snow Top anymore?"

Marlon shook his head. "Months now. She don't know I'm alive."

"Too bad. You really had it made there, kid." He

smacked his lips. "That was one babe that knew what she wanted and was willing to go all the way to get it." He took two cigars from his breast pocket, held one out to Marlon, drew a shake of the head. "What happened?"

"Allen put his foot down. Gave it a couple of weeks' play and then ruled it off."

The plugger bit the end off his cigar, spat it at the floor. "I don't blame him. It wasn't too good a disc." He rolled the cigar between thumb and forefinger in the center of his lips. "Funny thing, that babe can really sell a number. But you've got to be watching her when she does or it don't get to you."

The orchestra made a brave attempt at a fanfare. A curtain at the far end of the floor was pulled aside and a tall, full-blown redhead stood in the doorway. She wore a beaded gown, long bottle-green gloves and carried a parasol. As she came onto the dance floor the band began an indifferent rendition of "Lady of the Evening."

As she started across the floor the expression on her face was angelically pure, but she managed to give her body a motion that started her full breasts flowing and swaying in the loose bodice of her gown. When she reached the front of the dance floor she swung around and walked back. Her hips worked slowly and tantalizing against the soft fabric of the gown. When she reached the doorway, she tossed the parasol aside, turned, and stood for a moment, a smile on her lips. Then she stripped off the gloves, pulled a pin from the neck of the gown, and let it sag open.

Now the band stepped up the tempo. She half-danced, half-strutted across the floor, pulling pin after pin until the gown hung open to her waist. She strutted around the floor, her breasts, like something alive, swaying in and out of the gown. This time when she reached the door, she slid the gown back over her shoulders and stepped out of it.

The whiteness of her body gleamed in the spotlight. Her legs were long, sensuously shaped. Full, rounded thighs curved into high-set hips, which swelled excitingly before narrowing to her waist. The flimsiest possible brassiere made a half-hearted attempt to cover the full breasts, a beaded fringe hung from her hips.

The drummer, his face gleaming with sweat, his lips moving spasmodically, started to beat out a primitive rhythm that set the hairs on Marlon's neck on end.

The redhead started to undulate in the middle of the floor. Her hands started at the side of her thighs, came up slowly, palms smoothing the skin over her hips, slid over her stomach, and up under her breasts, cupping them. Her shoulders started to sway in rhythm to the drum. She ran her palms up along her neck to her hair, released it and let it flow down over her shoulders in a coppery cascade.

The room suddenly seemed charged with electricity as the drummer picked up the tempo. The redhead's body started to twist and squirm, undulating with feverish intensity from shoulders to ankles. As the trumpet picked up the beat, her twisting and squirming became more frenetic until the music hit a shattering peak, then died away to a silence that seemed to shatter the eardrums. She stood in the middle of the floor, then tore off her brassiere as she let out a frenzied scream.

The lights suddenly went down, and when they came up the floor was empty. The faces of the customers at the adjoining tables gleamed wetly in the reflected light.

Eddie Marlon swabbed at his forehead with a balled

handkerchief. "That's quite a woman."

Shannon nodded, yanked the unlighted cigar from between his teeth, ruefully studied the mangled end. "I ought to know better than to chew on a cigar while that babe's on." He licked a loose leaf back into place, replaced the cigar between his teeth. "You never caught her act before?"

The thin man shook his head. "I don't get over this way often. Usually the East Side."

Shannon nodded. "It's easier on the nerves over there. But I had a special reason for bringing you over here."

Marlon grinned. "That's reason enough," he nodded toward the floor. "I'm going to stick around for the late show. I've got to see what this babe does for an encore."

"I thought you'd go for her. But it's strictly look, no touch." He scratched a wooden match, touched it to his cigar. "She belongs to a big shot in the Teamsters Union. A guy who carries a lot of muscle. And he knows how to use it."

"Maybe she'll have a night off."

Shannon grinned bleakly. "With all the stuff available, don't go getting your head shot off for one you can't get."

"I hear a lot about all this available stuff, but I don't get to see much of it," Marlon complained. "Besides, it takes real moolah to run in that league and Allen isn't passing out that kind of dough."

"That's why I brought you over here."

Marlon looked interested. "Why?"

"Maybe I know a way to throw some of that kind of dough your way." He took the cigar from between his lips, studied the thin collar of white ash, tapped it off. "Arnie Cohen, A and R man for Rhythm, had a date down the street. He's going to drop by here after it."

"What's A and R man mean?"

"Hell! He's the Artists and Repertoire chief at Rhythm. He decides what artist does what number. He's got a little idea he wants to talk over with you."

"What kind of an idea?"

Shannon shrugged. "It'd be better to let him tell you."

And Eddie Marlon had to be satisfied with that. They sat through the rest of the show—a couple of overaged strippers who looked pathetic in their efforts to appear seductive, a couple of queers in what was intended to be a burlesque of an adagio dance, and a blues singer who closed the show with a cracked, whisky-coarsened voice.

It was a little after 12:30 when Arnie Cohen arrived. He slid into the chair opposite Eddie Marlon, seemed too big to fit on it. He was fat, soft-looking; his eyes were two black, shiny marbles almost lost in the puffy rolls of fat. Dark, damp ringlets made a futile effort to cover the bald spot that gleamed pinkly through them.

"Hope I didn't keep you boys waiting too long." His voice was blubbery, as though choked by the fat that hung from his jowls. He studied Eddie Marlon from behind heavily veined eyelids. "Shannon's been telling me how much help you been, Eddie. We appreciate it."

"I like to do favors for my friends," the thin man told him cautiously.

Cohen's head bobbed, disturbing the rolls of fat under his chin. "That's the kind of talk I like to hear. And that's why we want to do something for you." He leaned back, laced his fingers over his stomach. His knuckles were dimples. "We're doing a pressing on a number, 'Cloud of Cotton,' that's going to hit a million.

It's going to need some help, of course, but it's a real solid job." His little eyes darted from Eddie to the plugger and back. "Brett Lyons's ork doing the background and Dinah Reed the vocal."

Marlon whistled softly. "That's real big-league stuff. You won't need any help with that."

"We don't need it, but we want it," the A and R man told him. "Taos Recording did a side on the number with a small combo. We're going to cover their side with a big-league job and I want to snowball this disc until we really clobber them."

"I didn't think that side was going places," Marlon shrugged. "We've been giving it a little whirl, but nothing sensational."

"That's because Taos Recording is a schlock outfit. No promotion, no get-behind. That we got. Plenty." He grunted as he dug his fat hand into his breast pocket, brought out a sheaf of papers, riffled through them. "Take my word, that number's a sleeper. Put a name on the label, it's headed for the top." He selected a folded page of newsprint. "Here's the *Variety* list of the most-played discs for the week." He held it out, indicating a line with a stubby finger. "Baltimore, Washington. 'Cloud' is going good."

"That could be a plant, Arnie," Shannon protested cautiously. "Give me a couple of yards in some of those markets and I can come up with all the most-played listings you want."

"A big outfit, they might do it. Taos Recording? No." The fat man shook his head, disturbing the rolls of fat. "It's a real sleeper, this number. With a backing like we're going to give it, it could become number one in the country."

Marlon studied the list, nodded. "That little combo that waxed it for Taos is doing real good with it. My boss likes it, but I wasn't so hot for it."

Cohen took back the *Variety* page, folded it up, stuck it in his pocket. "That's where you can do us a favor. Your boss likes the song? Good. Just use the Dinah Reed waxing." He spread his pouting lips in an ingratiating smile. "You co-operate with us and vice versa."

Eddie Marlon made a production of finding a cigarette, fitting it to the corner of his mouth. "How do you co-operate with me?"

"How much money do you make with Allen? Not much, eh?"

"Maybe I'm satisfied." A cold note crept into the little man's voice.

Cohen reached out, laid his hand on the other's sleeve. "Please. You mustn't misunderstand. I'm not prying, believe me. I want to help." He removed the hand, leaned back. "The point I'm trying to make is that no matter how much you're making with Allen another bill a week wouldn't hurt. Am I right?"

"A hundred a week? For what?"

The fat man shrugged. Bubbles formed and broke at the corners of his lips. "For co-operating with us. You get us two plays a day of our waxing of 'Cloud,' you forget the Taos waxing, and you collect a bill a week." He raised his hands, palms upward. "It's that simple."

Marlon looked from the fat man to the plugger.

"You're always moaning about what you could do with a couple of extra dollars," Shannon told him. "I tossed this proposition at Arnie and he went for it."

"Suppose I can't produce? Suppose Allen spots the switch and nixes it?"

"That's your end of the proposition. You can't produce, you say so and we have another drink and forget all about it." The heavy eyelids hooded the fat man's eyes. "But if you take the proposition, I expect you to go through with it. I have commitments too."

"If it was my own show—"

Cohen nodded. "In that case, we got no problem. But with Allen, it's a different story." He turned to Shannon. "By the way, what's with him and that platinum blonde? You know the one, she waxed—"

Shannon shot a warning look at the fat man, cut him off.

"Wait a minute." Marlon turned to the plugger. "Jo Leary? Allen been playing house with her?"

"Look, kid. All I know is that word's around she's hooked herself a meal ticket. The disc laid an egg, she bowed out of the Shamrock. Somebody's lifting the hot for a Park Avenue setup."

"What about Allen?"

Shannon shrugged. "She's seen around the better spots a lot with him. So that's their business, no, kid?"

"The mealy-mouthed sonofabitch! He warns me off stuff like that so he can move in himself." He turned back to Cohen. "Okay, mister, I'm your boy. I'll see to it that the Dinah Reed waxing gets the play. How, I don't know. Or maybe I do."

The fat man's hand was soft and wet when they shook on the deal.

Arnie Cohen wasn't as soft as he looked. He had made it the hard way from song plugger to A and R man and there were very few holds he didn't know. In some quarters it was whispered that he had written the book.

He had been the first of the A and R men to see the possibilities of an antiquated copyright law that gave anyone the right to make a mechanical recording of any song as long as he paid two cents a copy royalty. Now he could sit back and wait for another recording company to take the initial expense of a waxing on an untried number, and then if it looked like a success, he stepped in with a cover recording on it with a name star and band from his stable. In that way he could guarantee to turn out enough hits to justify his job, and still shake down the publishers with no fear that a big one might slip by him.

In return, he was on the receiving end from the orchestra leaders and the vocalists who wanted him to assign them potential hits.

"It's a filthy racket," old Leo Marcus of Tune Music Co. snapped at him when Arnie set a $1,000 tab on the recording of one of Marcus's songs. "By keeping my song off a record, you're killing my sheet-music sale."

The fat man lolled back in his chair, studied the publisher coldly. "All you old-timers are the same. Always complaining that somebody's taking advantage of you. Maybe that schmaltz you're peddling is the trouble. Maybe it would go twenty years ago, but today it's from nowhere. Why should I take the hot for finding out?"

"Twenty years ago this song would be published without my having to kick back to guys like you."

The fat man shrugged. "I been hearing that since I got in this business. You old-timers started the payola by laying it on the line for singers and bands—"

"You're crazy."

"Yeah? Then how come a guy like Al Jolson who never wrote a line in his life has his name on fifty, sixty songs? Because he got behind them, that's why, and you guys cut him in!"

The old man stared at the fat man incredulously. "You mean to sit there and compare yourself with a Jolson or a Sophie Tucker? Sure they got behind a song. They did more than that. They made it. A Joley sings a song and the next day we sell a half a million copies."

Cohen squirmed uncomfortably in his chair, dropped his heavily veined lids to half mast. "So okay. We record a number and we sell a half a million copies, so where's the difference?" He reached over to the desk, picked up a pencil, rolled it between his thumb and forefinger. "You know the situation, Marcus. We got a long line of songs we're going to do. You want to wait until we reach yours, okay. After all, I got my company to think of—it costs between $500 and $1,000 to do a song right. You want to guarantee our costs—"

"Whose costs? Yours or the company's?"

Arnie Cohen pursed his lips, blew bubbles. "So maybe you better take it someplace else."

Leo Marcus finally placed his song with Continental Records, a small house. From the start it was apparent that he had a hit and the sales of records and sheet music started to climb.

Connie Wing, Cohen's assistant, burst into the fat man's office the next day. "You hear that song of Leo's that Continental waxed?"

The fat man nodded.

"It's going like hell, Arnie," Wing told him excitedly. "They got Johnny Diamond on it and he does a good job. I hear it's a real sleeper."

"You got a copy?"

"I can get one."

"Take it down to Sam, have him do an arrangement. They got Johnny Diamond?" He closed his eyes, considered. "So okay, we'll do it with Brett Lyons and we'll use Laurie Evans for the vocal."

His assistant whistled soundlessly. "That'll clobber the Diamond side. But what if Leo won't stand still for us doing a cover?"

The fat man opened his eyes. "You mean he's got a choice? You never heard of the 1909 copyright law?"

Wing shook his head.

Arnie Cohen grinned. "It says anybody can make a mechanical reproduction of a song just by paying two cents a copy."

"But that's all you have to pay if you do it in the first place."

The fat man closed his eyes again, nodded. "Coincidence, ain't it?"

"You mean we can make a cover on any record just by paying what we'd have to pay in the first place?"

"That's what the book says." Cohen grunted. "So instead of trying to understand it, get the Diamond side down to Sam. I want to get on it right away. Like you said, we'll clobber them."

It was Arnie Cohen's discovery of the gimmick in the copyright law that revolutionized the entire recording industry. Originally the gimmick had been inserted into the law to protect the small recording outfits from being forced to the wall by the big companies' gobbling up all the available material. Under Arnie Cohen's interpretation, it had directly the opposite effect—it made it possible for the big companies to sit back, force the publishers to pay tribute or go to the small companies. Then there was nothing to prevent the big companies from doing a cover on the number and using bigger and better name bands and vocalists so that their version became the standard and the original became forgotten.

6

The week following Eddie Marlon's meeting with Cohen, Marty Allen picked up the list of titles for the day's show, frowned at it. He flipped it back on the desk, leaned back in his chair. A dark bristle of beard blurred the outline of his chin. He customarily shaved during the five-minute news break at 7:30.

Eddie Marlon was busying himself at the huge record file at the far side of the room, his back to Allen. As he pulled a disc out far enough to read the label, he was aware of the heavier man's eyes on his back. He flipped the record back into place, turned around.

"Anything the matter?" There was a barely discernible note of truculence in his voice.

"I notice you've got Dinah Reed's 'Cloud' disc skedded for the 7:15 segment and again right after the nine o'clock news."

"It's a good side."

"Sure. So is the Taos waxing of 'Cloud.' We've been giving that the brush the past week or so."

Eddie shrugged, made a stab at nonchalance. "Why feed them a small-time artist, a small-time combo when we've got big-league stuff like Dinah Reed?"

The disc jockey tapped a cigarette from the pack on his desk, wet the end with the tip of his tongue, set it between his lips. "That the only reason?"

"What's that supposed to mean?"

"It's supposed to mean that I want to know if Arnie Cohen has you on the tit." Allen lighted the cigarette, took a deep drag, blew smoke from his nostrils. "I told you when you took the job that larceny was out. It still is."

Marlon tried to meet the other man's eyes, let his gaze fall first. "I don't know what you're talking about."

"Look, I let you get away with it with the Leary broad. Okay, I got a look at her and I don't blame you for wanting a piece of it. I also hear that you pick up a little change here and there for skedding certain titles. As long as they don't hurt anybody, I let them through. But this plugging a big-name cover is hurting the little combo that waxed 'Cloud' first. This I don't stand still for."

"Oh, sure. You're the friend of the people," Marlon snarled. "You're the little Lord Fauntleroy. You don't put the shake on. You do everything for no. Bull."

Allen stopped with the cigarette halfway to his lips. His eyes narrowed, a hard note crept into his voice. "I hope you can explain that, because if you can't, I'm going to throw you right down the elevator shaft. You made a crack, buster, now back it up."

"You think I don't know about you and Jo Leary?"

"What do you know?"

"You warn me off. You bust up my play by penciling her disc off the show. And why?"

"You tell me."

"Because you're trying to move in yourself, that's why. But you don't do anything obvious like plug her record. Not you. You go whole hog and set her up." Marlon's voice was shrill in his anger. "A guy in your spot, you could take your pick. But you got to move in on the only one I got."

Allen stuck the cigarette between his lips, inhaled deeply. He blew the smoke at the thin man who stood on the far side of the desk, trembling with rage. "You really think I've been on the make for Leary? Then you're a bigger jerk than I thought you were."

"Don't snow me, dad. You weren't as smart about it

as you think you were. You've been seen with her. Plenty."

"Alone?"

Marlon was about to continue his tirade, tripped over the question. "What do you mean alone? How the hell do I know if you were alone?"

"Then before you start shooting off that cottonpickin' mouth of yours, you ought to find out." He smoked in short, angry puffs. "Not that it's any of your damn' business, but I've never been alone with that broad in my life."

The anger drained out of Marlon's face. He stood staring at the man behind the desk with gaping mouth. "You never been alone with her? But you been with her. You been seen with her."

"Maybe that's why I was with her, kid. To be seen with her."

"I don't get it."

"Maybe I got elected to be the beard."

The thin man frowned. "The beard?"

"You never heard of a beard? I guess I've really got no right getting mad at a schnook like you. A beard's like this: a guy plays a babe and can't afford to get fingered for it, so he makes sure there's always another guy along. Anybody sees them figures maybe the babe's with the other guy. He's the beard."

"Oh." Marlon made an attempt to disguise how silly he felt. He reached across the desk, picked up the pack of cigarettes. "Okay?"

"Be my guest." Allen watched while the thin man attempted to regain his composure by making a production of lighting the cigarette.

"You going to fire me?"

Allen shrugged. "What would *you* do?"

The thin man nodded. "I guess I don't blame you. I

guess you figure I'm pretty dumb."

"Not as dumb as you seem to think I am."

"What do you mean?"

"The deal with Cohen. What are you getting for the heavy play you've been giving the 'Cloud' disc?"

"A bill a week for two plays a day."

"You know how I feel about being on the tit."

"I got hustled." Marlon shrugged weakly. "They put the burn on me about you moving in on Leary. It's the first time—"

"And the last."

"If you give me another chance. Look, Marty, this job means a lot to me. It's the first time I ever had a chance to do something I like, to be around the kind of people I heard about and read about. Give me another chance, will you, Marty?"

"Look, kid, maybe I'm hipped on this subject. But records can be awfully important to the music business in the next couple of years—if guys like Arnie Cohen will let them. But if he keeps trying to stack the deck he's going to louse up radio just like guys like him have loused up the band business and the juke boxes."

A boy in a dingy white jacket appeared in the doorway. "Got some coffee for you, Mr. Allen." He walked in, deposited two stained containers on the desk top. "Murph says you didn't show this morning, he figures maybe you need it by now."

Allen grinned, dug into his pocket for a bill, passed it to the boy. "Tell Murph thanks. I had a couple of things on my mind this morning." He pulled a container toward him, indicated the other. "Have some coffee, kid."

Marlon sheepishly picked up the container, rolled it between his palms. "How about it, Marty? Do I get another chance?" He shrugged. "I know I've been a jerk. Don't be sore at me."

Allen gouged the top from his container. "I guess I shouldn't be, at that. Guys with a lot more experience in this business than you get taken in by sharpies like Arnie Cohen. He's got a lot of the what-with behind him and he doesn't mind spending." He swirled the hot coffee around in the container. "Suppose I do give you another chance. What about the deal on the 'Cloud' disc?"

"The deal's off. Like you said."

"Arnie don't mind spending, kid, but he expects to get what he buys." Allen looked up, squinted. "He can get real unreasonable when he don't get it."

"I'm not afraid of him."

"How much of his dough have you taken?"

"A bill."

The disc jockey nodded. "That calls for two plays a day for a week. That what you said?" When the thin man nodded, Allen continued, "Okay, so he's got two more days' play coming. We'll give it to him. That's the end of it. Understand?"

Marlon nodded miserably. "Thanks, Marty."

"The only reason I'm doing it is I'm allergic to coming in here this early in the morning to look at a guy with a hole in his head, that's all." He stared at the thin man for a moment. "I'm bailing you out on this one, kid, because I think you really got had. If I thought you really had larceny in your heart, this'd be it. But it's the last time."

"You're the boss, Marty." Eddie hooked a chair, pulled it to him, sank into it. "Mind me asking something?"

Allen took a gulp from his container, shook his head. "How come you got to be a beard for anybody?"

"I didn't have to. The guy's a friend of mine. He had something to lose by being tied up with Leary. I didn't, so I went along with it."

Marlon eyed the disc jockey curiously. "You seem pretty anxious to cover for this friend of yours. Anybody I know?"

The man behind the desk grinned at him bleakly. "None of your business, kid. And if I were you, I wouldn't make any special effort to find out."

"But why the big deal? Hiding behind you? Suppose your wife gets to hear about it?"

"Annie knows the whole story. My friend's married but doesn't work at it, and his wife doesn't particularly care what he does as long as it doesn't get into the papers."

Marlon nodded. "I get it."

"Cohen knows the picture, too, kid. He was just trying to steam you."

"If it means so much to your friend, why don't Arnie put the heat on him? From the way you're willing to front for him, it looks like he could get to you a lot faster than I can."

"Cohen would love to. But he'd have a tough time making it stick, and if he goofed on it, my friend might be mad enough to really go to work on Arnie." He shook his head, drained his container, and crushed it in his palm. "Arnie's too smart to go up against anything he mightn't be able to walk away from."

"So he uses me as the patsy."

"Don't take it too big, kid." Allen grinned at him. "He figured it wouldn't cost anything to try, so he tried. You went for it, so he picks up the pot. If you didn't go for it, he'd try to get under your skin some other way. Arnie doesn't give up very easily!"

"I'll remember that."

"I'd better get at these commercials and get organized." Marty glanced up at the clock on the wall over the control booth. "We haven't got much time."

Marlon smoked quietly, watched the disc jockey rewriting the typewritten copy from the agency. "I notice you've been doing a lot of rewriting on that stuff lately, Marty."

The man behind the desk scowled at the typewritten copy, shook his head. "It's too damn' stuffy for this time of the morning. These characters at the agency are in love with words." He continued to slash at the paper with a soft pencil, frowning in his concentration. He scribbled a rewrite at the bottom of the page to be inserted in the deleted portion, reread it, and seemed satisfied. "You don't have to hit a customer with a sledge hammer to make him buy. Sometimes it's easier to tickle him into it with a feather."

"I got a big charge out of the way you gagged up that elevator shoes commercial yesterday. Get any kickback on it?"

Allen shook his head, didn't look up from the typewritten copy. "The boys at the agency weren't too happy, but when they found out the sponsor got a big kick out of it, they backed down."

"Yeah, but making the customers laugh at his product—"

The disc jockey finished with the commercial, set it aside, and leaned back. "They weren't laughing at us, kid, they were laughing *with* us. It makes a big difference." He glanced at the clock, reached for a cigarette. "You have to know where to draw the line. You can kid all you want as long as you don't kid the integrity of the product or the people who make it. Anything else you can poke fun at."

Marlon was about to prolong the conversation, noticed the engineer and the director filing into the booth. They waved to him, started getting ready for the show. Marlon scurried back to the record files, began pulling out discs for the show. He felt guilty as he pulled out the Dinah Reed waxing of "Cloud"; just two more days and then they'd go back to the original Taos version.

7

Marty Allen had come to radio from a now defunct theatrical weekly called *Zit's*. He had written a column called "In Tin Pan Alley" and had built himself a reputation for his knowledge of music and his gentle handling of the subjects of his weekly criticism.

The first time he saw Ann Constance was from the third row of Loew's State where she was appearing with one of Ed Sullivan's Dawn Patrol revues in which the *Daily News* columnist was first breaking in the dead-pan delivery for which he was to become famous years later.

Ann Constance was tall, redheaded and Canadian. She sold a song with a husky voice that played on Allen's spine like a xylophone. At the end of the show he worked his way backstage, and through the good graces of the State's manager, Al Rosen, he met her.

It was a whirlwind courtship that ended in marriage at St. Malachy's three years later. Just about that time, John K. Dickenson of Station WTLO had hit upon the idea of setting up a wake-up program with someone to play music and keep an eye on the clock for the million or more listeners the station had won for itself in the metropolitan market.

Marty Allen was a natural choice for the spot, both because he knew the music business backward and because he had a pleasant voice and manner.

The program was over five years old and something of a fixture in Radio Row when Joe Devine steered Eddie Marlon to him. Marty had mixed feelings about the kid from the start. He was aware of Marlon's resentment that it was Marty Allen and not Eddie Marlon who ran the program. He couldn't help knowing that Marlon despised him for not cashing in on the program's potential.

But with it all, he couldn't help feeling sorry for the kid with his greedy ambitions, with his never-ending eager-beaver drive. On the few occasions when he had caught Eddie using the program to plug the songs of a special performer or of a special company he had called him on it. It wasn't until he became aware that Arnie Cohen was beginning to take a special interest in the kid that Marty felt called upon to have a showdown. Like most people in the music business, Marty knew of the influence Cohen was beginning to wield, had some insight into the changes that a man like Cohen could make in the business.

It was shortly after the showdown with Marlon that Marty Allen and his wife walked into Al and Dick's, a popular spot with the music crowd. He waved across the room to Del Shaft of Taos and a group of Taos's pluggers, then settled for a booth at the far side of the room. They had just ordered Martinis when Bud Cole of Cole Music crossed the room, slid in alongside Marty.

"How are you, Mrs. Allen?" he asked the redhead.

"Fine, Bud."

Cole turned his attention to Marty Allen. "What do you hear around, Marty?"

Allen shrugged. "You didn't come over to hear what I know, you came over to tell me something you know." He grinned. "What's on your mind?"

"Murder. This business keeps getting more cutthroat every day." He took his arms off the table while the waiter slid Martinis in front of Allen and his wife. "Bring me one, too, Harry." When the waiter headed back toward the bar, Cole went on, "These A and R men are really putting the arm on us. Heavy."

"The old payola, eh? I've been hearing a lot about it lately."

The redhead frowned. "The which?"

"The payola," the publisher told her. "The kickback. It's away out of hand, Ann. You either go along with it or your stuff gathers dust on the shelves." He turned to Allen. "I got a sure-fire hit. Of course it don't mean a thing to me unless I get it recorded, so I go to Arnie Cohen with it. He says okay, he likes it. That's two months ago. What happens? Nothing."

"Why?" Ann turned from the publisher to her husband. "If it's a good number, why should he sit on it?"

"He's waiting Bud out. There'll be a fee to get the number on a platter. If Bud doesn't come through and has to get someone else to do the song, then Cohen will wait to see how it goes, and if it looks real good, he'll record it with one of his top names."

"Well, is that bad?"

"It's not good," Cole told her. "All we get out of it is two cents on every record, and we have to split that with the writer. A cover job might sell, but it might also kill what could have been a runaway. If we could pick and choose who was going to do our songs—"

"Why can't you?" Ann wanted to know.

"Because we have no control over mechanical reproduction. Anybody can record any of our songs if they pay us the two cents. That's why today the publisher is beginning to be strictly nothing in this business."

"You mean you publish a song and if it's a hit anybody can put it on a record? Without your permission?"

The waiter was back with the Martini; Cole waited until he was out of earshot. "With my permission or without my permission he can record my song."

"But that's insane. In the theater, when one producer has a hit every other producer can't just put on a production, can he?"

Cole shook his head. "Just in this business." He sipped at his drink, made a wry face. "In the theater when a writer has a good play, he doesn't go out and put it on himself, does he?"

"Well, not often."

"In this business, everybody produces. You get a singer who's hot, he publishes songs and he only sings what he publishes. You ask him to get behind one of your songs and you either got a partner or he tells you he's too busy with his own numbers. You want a record cut by a big house, all of a sudden the A and R man is your partner. It's murder."

Allen looked thoughtful. "Is it really that bad, Bud?"

"You got no idea. It ain't like the old days when we'd work on a song, plug it and then make sixteen cents a copy on sheet music. Today, you get something that's hot, the disc jockeys play it so hard and so often that by the time you get your sheet music distributed, it's old stuff."

"What are you fellows going to do about it?" Allen wanted to know.

Cole shrugged. "What can we do? It's getting worse instead of better. It's got so, instead of us being able to put our numbers in front of the public by getting some band or singer to front them, now the A and R men decide what the public hears and what it don't hear."

"You can still promote through bands, can't you?"

Cole shrugged. "With radio today you hit a thousand people for every one you used to hit in night clubs and restaurants. And the bands, they know what side their bread's buttered on. Why should they get behind a number if the A and R man they're tied up with won't cut a record on it?"

"It sounds pretty grim," Allen conceded.

"Well, you didn't come in here so I could spoil your appetite." The publisher grinned ruefully. "I guess it's just that we have to depend on guys like you to keep it from getting any worse." He finished his drink, set the glass down. "I wish there were more guys like you in the business, Marty. You know the music business from away back. Not like a lot of these guys that spin records and make with the funny talk on some stations. I wish there were more like you." He got out of the booth, shoved his hand at Allen. "Keep it clean, kid."

After Cole had gone back to his table, Ann turned to her husband. "Is it really that bad?"

Allen nodded. "My guess is that the next ten years or so will see the record people taking over the music business. Independents like Bud Cole will be forced to the wall. They'll either have to shell out more than they can afford to get their songs recorded, or else they'll have to sit back and watch the crooks and the shysters get all the plug and promotion."

"Can't you do something to help them?"

Allen grinned, shook his head. "What can I do? I'm just a little deejay. I try to give as many of the small guys a break as I can, but don't forget that I can't play a record unless there is a record."

"It's a filthy shame, Marty."

"It's all of that. Hell, even this kid I've got working for me, this Eddie Marlon, they've been working on him. I've got to keep one eye on him and one eye on the schedule to make sure I don't stiff the little guys who did the original waxing in favor of the covers from outfits like Rhythm with the big names."

"I never realized what they were up against. I figured they licensed a company to record their song and then sat back to cash in on the royalties."

Allen picked up his glass, twisted the thin stem between his thumb and forefinger. "As Bud said, that's not where the publishers make their money. They make it from sheet music—sixteen cents a copy, or whatever the figure is now, as against two cents on a record. And the way a record gets a rush when Rhythm or one of the big houses gets behind it, it burns the song out before they can sell enough sheet music to pay the printer."

"But he must be exaggerating about men like Arnie Cohen. Surely they couldn't keep their jobs if they passed up really good songs and just published the junk they get paid off on."

"Well, by covering on hit records, they manage to keep their sales figures high enough to cover their salaries, I guess." He signaled the waiter. "It's a far cry from the days when I first started covering Tin Pan Alley for *Zit's*, that's for sure."

The redhead slid her hand across the table, covered his with it. "You'll keep on doing what Bud Cole asked, won't you, Marty?"

"What's that?"

"Keep it clean."

He winked at her. "Sure. Anyway, I'm allergic to mink. It makes my eyes water."

"That's funny"—the redhead grinned back—"it makes my mouth water."

It was in Eddie Marlon's third year with Marty Allen that it happened. The pealing of the phone at his ear was shrill, discordant. Eddie Marlon groaned, cursed softly, dug his head into the pillow, but the noise refused to go away. He opened one eye experimentally, peered at the half-drawn shade, noted that it was bright daylight. The clock on the night table made the time to be 3:40. He hadn't got to bed until after 2.

He snaked one arm from under the covers, grabbed the receiver, lifted it off the hook.

"Eddie? This is Allen."

The man in the bed groaned. "I just got to bed, Marty. Why the hell are you calling at this hour?"

"Trouble, kid. I need you. How soon can you get over to Park and 56th?"

Eddie tried to wipe the sleep from his eyes, but it wouldn't wipe. "The way I feel, about a year."

"This is serious, kid. It's a real jam." The voice on the phone hesitated a moment. "I'm in a spot where I've got to move fast."

"What's it about anyway?"

"Jo Leary." Allen was silent for a second. "Look, kid, I've got no choice. I've got to take a chance. You have to stand up for me on this one."

"But, Marty—"

Allen interrupted. "I stood up for you when the cards were down. You work with me on this and you won't be sorry. I just hope I won't be."

"What's the matter with Leary?"

"She's hurt bad. Real bad. She may go out on me."

Marlon was suddenly awake. And ice cold. "What'd you say?"

"I said get the hell over here. This can be real nasty."

"The cops know?"

There was a pause. "No. I'm trying to figure some

way to handle it so they don't have to know."

"Where do I come?"

"Denton Apartments. Penthouse B."

"I'll be right over." The thin man dropped the receiver back on its hook, started stuffing his legs into his pants. He headed for the bathroom, finished the waking-up process by dashing cold water onto his face. He was headed for the lobby of his hotel and a cab less than fifteen minutes after he received the call.

The Denton Apartments was an expensive pile of stone and plate glass that towered over Park Avenue at the southwest corner of 56th Street. The lobby was furnished in aggressively modernistic style. Brightly colored couches and chrome tables tastefully complemented the soft, restful, ankle-deep pastel carpeting.

Eddie Marlon plowed through the deep pile rug to the elevator bank set in the rear of the lobby. He jabbed at the button marked *Penthouse*, chafed at the slow progress the cage made upward. The elevator glided to a smooth stop, the doors slid noiselessly open. He crossed the small hallway, pushed the button next to the door on which a gilt *B* was stenciled.

The door opened a crack, "Who is it?" It was Allen's voice.

"Me, Marty. Eddie."

The door swung open; Allen caught his arm, pulled him inside, and closed the door after him. The bigger man led the way through a small lobby into a cheerfully furnished combination living-room and den. To the left, a huge picture window looked out onto a hedge-lined terrace.

A man with rumpled white hair sat in a big armchair, his face in his hands. He looked up as Eddie entered, studied him with red-rimmed eyes.

Jo Leary had dyed her hair again. She lay on a sling

chair that faced the picture window. She wore only a tight pair of toreador pants, her face was turned to the back of the chair. A startlingly white, unsunburned strip cut across the cocoa color of her tan, a number of bright red strips ribboned the rest of her back.

"She dead?"

Allen stopped in front of the girl, put the tips of his fingers to the side of her throat. "No."

The man in the chair had returned his face to his hands, seemed oblivious to what was happening.

"What the hell happened?" Marlon wanted to know.

Allen reached over to the floor at the end of the couch, picked up a plaited whip. "I guess they got playing games and he didn't know his own strength." He looked over to where the man sat. "It could be an awful stink." He tossed the whip on the coffee table. "If it gets out."

"If it gets out? How you going to stop it?" Marlon grunted. "Especially if she dies?"

Allen started pacing the floor nervously. "Look, kid, I'm going to level with you. You know who this is?" He stopped alongside the white-haired man. "John K. Dickenson, president of Republic Broadcasting."

The man in the chair raked his fingers through his hair, didn't look up.

Marlon whistled noiselessly. "The big boss. I'll say it could cause a stink. This'll push everything off the front pages for a month."

Allen resumed his pacing. "We can't let it happen."

The girl moaned; the disc jockey hurried to her side, made her comfortable. "Okay, baby?"

"My back," she moaned. "It's on fire."

"It'll be all right. Just a little while, baby." He brushed the hair back out of her face, looked up. "This kid has to get to a hospital."

"You mean you haven't called an ambulance?"

Allen got up, brushed off his knees. "We got a house doctor up. He put something on the cuts to kill the pain." He plucked at his nose with thumb and fore-finger. "Kid, you're pretty hep. I've got a proposition for you."

Marlon's eyes narrowed. "I don't think I'm going to like this."

"Mr. Dickenson can't get mixed up in this. For lots of reasons—"

"Far as I can see he's in it up to his eyeballs." Marlon grunted.

"—he's an important figure in radio, he's an impor-tant figure in the community." Allen plowed ahead as though he hadn't heard the interruption. "But most important of all, he's a married man and both he and his wife are very prominent. Like you said, a natural for the front pages of the tabs."

"He should've remembered that."

"All right, all right. So he should have remembered. He didn't and we're in a jam." Allen walked over to a console radio, picked a cigarette from a dish, tapped it on the console with his back to the thin man. "We've got to supply a stand-in for the boss on this rap."

Marlon stared at the other man's back with his mouth agape. "You're using words, but you're not get-ting to me. You mean—"

Allen swung around. "I mean you've got a chance to do yourself a lot of good. You be here when the am-bulance comes, take the blame—"

"For what?"

"I told you we'd make it up to you," Allan snapped. "This is no time to dicker."

"But suppose she dies?"

"She won't if you stop talking so damn much and

give us a chance to get her into a hospital." He jammed the cigarette into his mouth, touched a lighter to it. "What've you got to lose?"

Marlon considered, walked to the picture window, stared out over the city. He was unmarried, had no ties. If the girl recovered, she could be prevailed upon to refuse to press charges; and he would be in a position to demand plenty of concessions. But if she died—

"Come on, kid," Allen pressured. "I've got to get the boss out of here. What do you say?"

The man at the window took his time turning around. "Suppose I do take this rap? How do I know he'll stand by me if the kid dies?"

Allen groaned. "What choice does he have? Besides, she's not going to die." He walked over to the chair, put his fingers to the girl's carotid. "When I first got here I could hardly feel a pulse, now it's almost normal. But the kid needs care. Fast."

Marlon considered, nodded. "Okay. I'll take the fall. But I come high."

Allen bobbed his head. "We'll take care of you." He rushed over to the white-haired man, caught him by the arm, and pulled him to his feet. "Come on, Mr. Dickenson, we've got to get out of here. Eddie's going to take care of everything for us."

The white-haired man's eyes turned toward the couch. "My wife—"

"Your wife'll never hear a thing about it." Allen looked around, spotted the man's jacket over the back of a chair, propelled him over to it and helped him put the jacket on. "You better put in the call for the ambulance, kid."

Marlon nodded, walked to the telephone, dialed the operator. While he waited, he watched Allen checking the place to make sure no sign of Dickenson's presence was left.

"Number please?" a metallic voice demanded.

"There's been an accident, operator. We need an ambulance."

"One moment, please." There was a click, a buzz and then a man's voice asked, "What's the address on the emergency?"

"Penthouse B, Denton Apartments. Park and 56th."

"We'll have a bus right over," the voice assured him.

Marlon dropped the receiver back onto its cradle, watched Allen helping the white-haired man to the door. "Wait a minute, Marty," he called. He walked over to the coffee table, picked up the plaited whip, held it out. "Maybe you'd better take this with you. Maybe Mr. Dickenson doesn't feel dressed without it."

The girl on the chair was softly moaning her way back to consciousness when a rap on the door announced the arrival of the police.

"You call for an ambulance here, mister?"

Marlon nodded, stood aside, waited until the patrolman had entered. He led the way to the living-room.

The cop's eyes widened at the sight of the girl. He bent down, examined the welts on her back, looked up at the thin man. "You?"

Marlon nodded, watched while the cop tugged a dog-eared leather notebook from his hip pocket. He found the stub of a pencil in his blouse.

"What's her name?"

"Jo Leary." He watched while the cop scribbled the name in his book. "Mine's Ed Marlon."

The cop looked around. "Who lives here?"

Marlon indicated the girl on the chair.

"How'd it happen?"

Marlon shrugged. "We were fooling around. I guess I didn't know my own strength." He walked over to the console and picked out a cigarette. "I hope you can keep this quiet, officer."

"Why?" The cop studied him, seemed unimpressed.

"Miss Leary's a singer. She's due for a build-up at Republic Broadcasting. It could cost them important money if she got mixed up in a scandal."

"How about you?"

Marlon shrugged. "I'm just a messenger at Republic. Work in the music library. Nobody's going to get excited over me."

There was a ring of the doorbell, the cop went to open it. An ambulance attendant and a young intern came in. The cop led them to the girl.

The intern examined the girl's back, looked up at the cop quizzically. The cop nodded. "Games."

The intern looked over to where Marlon stood smoking. "From the looks of the babe's back, I'd say they were playing for keeps. You going to report this?"

"You're damned right," the cop growled.

"I would if I were you. She seems to be reacting normally, but she's suffered a severe shock. She could die."

Eddie Marlon gave no outward sign of the sinking feeling in the pit of his stomach. He had a sneaking suspicion that he might have been suckered. It was his word against an important man like the president of Republic Broadcasting and there was plenty to tie him to the girl. His hand shook imperceptibly as he placed the cigarette between his lips.

The intern was still ministering to the girl when the cop led him to the elevator and to the waiting patrol car.

8

Jo Leary was immediately placed on the critical list at Roosevelt Hospital and no one but her attorney was permitted to see or question her during a three-day period. The incident had attracted relatively little attention. Neither of the parties involved was sufficiently big to warrant more than a stick in the morning papers, although the *Mirror* did manage to dig up a centerfold photo of a heavily swathed figure being transferred to an ambulance at the corner of Park Avenue and 56th Street.

At the end of the three-day period, when her physician felt that she was able to answer questions, Jo Leary was visited by a team of plain-clothes men from the Detective Bureau. She immediately nailed any suggestions that the injuries were anything but accidental; she said they were her own fault as a matter of fact. She had been rehearsing a new production number in which she was to portray a tigress. Her partner's stand-in, a minor employee of the broadcasting company for whom she was preparing a new show, had been a little overenthusiastic in his role of trainer. At any rate, there was no real damage done and the whole matter had best be forgotten.

Eddie Marlon received the news that no charges would be pressed from an attorney retained for him by John K. Dickenson. He strutted a little that evening when he showed at Lindy's for dinner, was even a little disappointed that the event hadn't created more of a splash than it did. Some of the wags at the tables nearby kidded him about his role in the affair, but most of those present hadn't even heard of it.

He stayed away from the studio for three days, laying his plans. Finally, about a week after the affair, he received a telephone call from Marty Allen.

"Where you been, kid?" the disc jockey asked.

"Where do you think? In the bastille! Or didn't you know?"

There was a brief silence. "Since then, I mean."

"Around."

"Look, kid, I don't know what's eating you, but there's no reason why you shouldn't come around. Matter of fact, our friend would like to tell you how much he appreciates your help."

"What's he got in mind?"

There was the brief pause again. "I don't think this is the place to discuss that, do you? Why don't you drop by in the morning and we'll talk it over as soon as I get off the air."

"That might be arranged."

"Good. Oh, and kid—don't worry about your salary. You're still on the pay roll."

Eddie Marlon sneered at the mouthpiece. "Gee, thanks." He tossed the receiver on its hook, walked to the window and stood looking west in the direction of roadway. A couple of years ago he was a punk kid carrying around a corny song he'd written, trying to get somebody to listen to it. Pretty soon now the positions would be reversed. They'd be coming to him with their songs, hats in their hands.

He had a couple of ideas he couldn't wait to put into practice.

John K. Dickenson had a suite of offices on the 56th floor of the skyscraper that housed the Republic Broadcasting Company's studio. A thick, wheat-colored broadloom stretched from the elevator to the double, ground-glass doors that bore in gold the information: *John K. Dickenson, Private.*

Eddie Marlon pushed open the doors into the outer office of the suite. A cool-looking blonde in a black wool dress sat behind a desk. She glanced up with no change of expression as Marlon came in.

"I'm Eddie Marlon. Dickenson is expecting me," he told her.

Her gray-green eyes flicked over him coolly. "I'll tell Mr. Dickenson you're here, Mr. Marlon." She manipulated the key on the intercom carefully as though to avoid damage to her highly shellacked nails. "Mr. Marlon is here, sir." A muted voice came back to her, she nodded. "Yes, sir."

When she stood up, Marlon could see she was much taller than he had expected. The black wool clung snugly to her ample curves as she walked to an inner door, held it open. She said, "He'll see you now, Mr. Marlon."

As Eddie brushed past her, his head was no higher than her shoulder. He could smell the expensive perfume she wore, and he couldn't help wishing he could get a look at her back. Or maybe Dickenson's peculiarities didn't extend to all his playmates.

As he entered the room the blonde closed the door behind him. It was a large room with a beamed ceiling, had a peculiar absence of sound, almost like a vacuum. The floor was covered with thick, gray-green carpeting, the leather furniture was polished to a soft gleam. One side of the room was covered by a huge bookcase, and in the center, facing the door, a highly polished desk dominated the room. Behind it, against the wall, a matching bar was topped by a group of framed plaques symbolizing awards.

A white-haired man whom he had difficulty recognizing as the same man he had seen in the Park Avenue apartment sat behind the desk, tapping it with spatulate fingers. Marty Allen stood at a far window looking out over the panoramic view of the city.

"Come in, Eddie." The man behind the desk worked at a note of cordiality in his voice, almost made it.

Marlon took his time about crossing the room, touched his hand to the white-haired man's briefly. From up close, Dickenson was distinguished-looking; his thick white hair was combed carefully into place, a polite smile fixed on his lips.

"Nice of you to come," he murmured.

At the window, Allen had turned. "Thought I'd see you at the studio this morning, kid," he chided gently.

Marlon nodded. "I was delayed." He walked over to an oversized leather chair, made himself comfortable. Allen permitted a brief frown to mar the smoothness of his brow, then he walked over and took a seat next to Dickenson. "Mr. Dickenson thought we ought to have this little talk and get things squared away."

The thin man nodded. He dug a pack of cigarettes out of his pocket, held it up. "All right to smoke?"

"Of course," the white-haired man said and worked on a smile, but it consisted mainly of an uptilting of the corners of his mouth. The wary expression in his eyes remained unchanged. "I feel that I owe you a considerable debt of gratitude, Eddie."

"I do, too." Marlon bent his head to touch a match to his cigarette, didn't fail to catch the startled glance exchanged between the other two. "What are we going to do about it?"

Dickenson pursed his lips. "Miss Leary is being very co-operative. As a matter of fact she's planning to do some traveling, and—"

"I don't like to travel."

"I see." The white-haired man couldn't keep the worried look from his eyes. "What do you like?"

"I like to work." The thin man took a deep drag on his cigarette, exhaled smoke through his nostrils. "I want a program of my own."

Marty Allen scowled. "A program? What kind?"

"A disc-jockey show."

"But we already have a disc jockey now. Marty's doing an outstanding job with it, and—"

"I don't want his job. I want afternoon time. Three to five."

A dull flush of color started at the collar of the man behind the desk. "Now, look here. I'm aware of what you did, and I'm aware that I owe you something—"

"Okay, you owe me something. That's what you owe me."

Dickenson was about to expostulate, but permitted Marty Allen to calm him down. "That's murder, kid. You can't make a disc-jockey show work at that hour. Who's going to listen to it? The women are done with their housework, nobody's driving home, and—"

"The kids."

"What?"

"You asked me who's going to listen to it. I'm telling you. The kids." Before they could interrupt, he continued, "Who fills the Paramount every time Frankie Sinatra or Perry Como plays the place? The housewives? The guys driving their cars? No! It's the kids. That's who'll listen to my show."

"It's ridiculous," Dickenson stormed. "That time's contracted for! Besides what do you know about running a disc-jockey show? We don't even know that you won't freeze up the first time you see a mike."

"Let me worry about that," Marlon told him. "And as for not knowing anything about running a show, I know more in a minute than your Golden Boy there knows in a year. Who do you think's been making contacts for his show for the last three years? Who's been skedding the releases? Me. All he's been doing is reading what gets shoved in front of him."

"Maybe you'd like my job, kid?" Allen chided gently.

"If I wanted it, I would have asked. And I would have got it," Marlon snapped. "I'm not here asking you for this spot. I'm telling you I expect you to clear it for me, and I don't care what it costs you!"

"You think you're riding pretty high, kid. Maybe if you were real smart—"

"If I was real smart I would have mailed this little item to the gossip columnists. Like to hear it?" He reached into his pocket, brought out an envelope, pulled out a typewritten note. He read: "*How come no one wondered how that chantoosie who was whipped in that Park Avenue apartment was able to pay the rent? Or did she? It certainly wasn't the kid who was arrested for the whipping—he's only an office boy at Republic.*" He folded the letter, returned it to the envelope.

The white-haired man jumped to his feet, stalked to the window. He stared out over the city, his hands locked behind his back. "What about it, Marty?"

Allen hadn't taken his eyes off the undersized man in the leather chair. "I guess he has us over a barrel, Mr. Dickenson." He grinned ruefully. "I wouldn't have believed it."

Marlon shrugged. "There's a payola due on everything, Marty. You plug a babe's song, she gets grateful and takes care of you. Somebody else gets paid off in cash. Me, I want a program."

"What happens if you can't make it go, kid? I haven't been in this business since yesterday. I'm telling you that as soon as the novelty wears off, your listeners are going back to the soap operas on the other nets and—"

"Then I'm strictly nowhere. I only charge one fare for each ride."

The man at the window turned. "How do I know that?"

Marlon shrugged. "How do I know that you won't turn off the juice before I can get the show on the road? You don't, except that I'm telling you."

Dickenson's shoulders sagged. He nodded. "It might be worth the try, Marty." He walked back to his desk, sank into his chair. "What do you plan to do with the time?"

Marlon had difficulty keeping his face expressionless, his voice matter-of-fact. "Records, chatter, personal interviews. Stuff that will build the most solid kid following in the business."

The white-haired man raked his fingers through his hair. "What good's a kid following? They don't buy anything. Who would you get for sponsors?"

"You haven't been reading the papers, Mr. Dickenson. There's a big change going on. Kids today aren't like they were before the war. They're getting the bit in their teeth, they're going to be running things. You want to know who'll fight to come in on this show?" He counted them off on his fingers. "Cosmetics, shampoos, record players, dancing lessons—"

He broke off as Marty Allen cocked his head, pursed his lips. "You know, Mr. Dickenson, there's just an outside chance he may have something. I've noticed one thing about my mail—what there is of it. More and more teen-agers have been writing in, fighting for plugs for their favorites. It's a cinch that a sponsor would find them plenty faithful."

Dickenson considered, came to a quick decision. "What do you want, specifically?"

"Clear the time between three and five. Put out announcements to the trade press and the columnists that we're planning a mammoth disc show to be beamed at teen-agers. Give me a month to line it up."

"What do we get in return?"

"One of the hottest shows in the country."

"I'm not talking about that. You know what I mean."

Marlon got up, sauntered over to the desk, deliberately crushed his cigarette in the big brass ash tray. "I want a year to make it or break it. At the end of that time, I'll sign one of two things; either a full confession that I did the job on Jo Leary, or a long-term contract with the station."

Dickenson looked from Marlon to Allen, drew an imperceptible nod. "All right, it's a deal." He made no effort to get up or shake hands as the thin man turned, walked from the room.

Rhythm Record Co. had its offices in the Brill Building, but the reception room alone was four times as large as the publisher on the fourth floor to whom Eddie Marlon had offered his song on his first visit to the building a little more than three years ago.

Huge framed photographs of important band leaders and vocalists adorned the walls, which were bathed with soft indirect lighting. Two large couches lined either wall; placed in the center of the room was a round table with a plant and some magazines, which Marlon had to circle to get to the railing that cut off the back of the room. Closed doors faced on the enclosed space.

Behind the railing were a receptionist's desk and a small switchboard.

The girl at the switchboard sat chewing on a wad of gum, watching his approach with no show of interest. The receptionist's desk was empty. He stopped near the gate in the railing. "Is Mr. Cohen in? Arnie Cohen?"

The girl at the switchboard didn't miss a beat on her gum. She had heavily mascaraed eyes, a poor job of bleach in her hair which left it dark at the roots. "Ain't seein' anyone today," she told him.

"How about Mike Shannon?"

"What's your name?"

"Eddie Marlon."

She did something at the board, muttered into the mouthpiece. "Take a seat. He'll be right out." She looked at her wristwatch, saw it was almost five, settled back with a sigh.

Marlon walked back to the round table, thumbed through the magazines. He had waited almost a half hour when one of the inner doors opened and the plugger walked out. "Come on in." He held the gate in the railing open. "Sorry to keep you waiting, kid."

"Any place we can talk?" Eddie wanted to know.

"One of the offices." He walked to one of the doors at the side of the waiting-room, opened it. A man looked up from his desk. Shannon closed it, opened another door and found the office empty. "Come on in here."

It was a small cubbyhole with the ever-present piano, a couple of hard-backed wooden chairs, and a desk.

"What's all the secrecy?" Shannon wanted to know.

"I got a program of my own."

Shannon raised his eyebrows. "What time?"

"Three to five every afternoon."

The plugger looked thoughtful, walked around the

desk, dropped into the chair. Mechanically, he picked a cigar from his breast pocket, stuck it between his teeth. "Two hours?" He shook his head. "That's a lot of time, kid. How come?"

Marlon shrugged. "I guess they finally recognized my talent."

"That's eight fifteen-minute slots. How you going to fill that?"

The thin man pulled a chair close to the desk, sat down. "Easy. I'm going to play records, old-timers and new releases for the first hour. Then, the next section I might have some live talent up there for an interview, maybe even do a song. Then I'm going to pick hits of the future."

The man behind the desk rolled the cigar from one corner of his mouth to the other. "They give you the green light for that?"

Marlon nodded. "I handle it any way I want."

"Three to five? Nobody's ever made a disc show work in that slot."

"That's because nobody's given any thought to how important the kids are to the music business. Who do you think makes a Sinatra or a Como? The kids."

Shannon got up, walked to the window, pushed it up a few inches, then walked back to the desk. "Maybe you got something there, kid."

"Sure I got something," Marlon said. "You help me get this on the road and there's enough for both of us."

Shannon looked undecided. "Sure, I'll help you all I can, kid. Anytime I have anything—"

"I don't mean that. I want you to work with me."

"I got a job. I couldn't just toss that up and—"

"You don't have to, at first. Working with me, you'll be doing your job. A helluva lot better than you can do it now." Marlon got up, leaned the palms of his hands on the desk. "Look, you don't want to spend the rest of your life stooging for Cohen, do you?"

"I don't know. It's a job. They're not too easy to get at my age."

"I can't figure a guy like you. You're all the time complaining that you spend half your life in boob traps trying to persuade some broken down band leader into playing your songs. Right?"

Shannon nodded unhappily, chewed on the unlighted cigar.

"Okay. So who hears it when they do play it? Some working stiff out on the town for a night. Some wolf on the make for a one-night stand with a broad. Some guy half in the bag romancing an out-of-town customer."

"It all helps."

Marlon shook his head irritably. "They're not going to remember the song. They're not going out to buy it. They hear it on my show, they will."

"Look, kid. I'm not playing down the importance of radio plugs. Why do you think I spend so much time polishing apples with guys like Allen? I just don't know if—"

"I do."

Shannon stared at the intense face of the man across the desk, nodded. "Okay. I'll listen. Maybe you got something I can use."

Marlon nodded his satisfaction, slid back into his chair. Then he pulled the chair so close to the desk his knees rubbed against it. "Remember that time Cohen made me a deal?"

The man behind the desk looked troubled. "Yeah, but I don't know if that would still hold, kid. He was hot on that side and—"

"I don't mean that particular disc. That was a long time ago. The point is there's always something he's hot on. Am I right?"

Shannon nodded.

"Okay. He's not the only A and R man in the business. They all get hot on a side and will go for plenty to get it a ride." He watched the older man's face. "We play along with that and it could get big. Real big."

Shannon nodded cautiously. "It could get."

The little man relaxed. "That's where you come in."

"What's where I come in?"

"You handle the outside contact for me. Set up the plays. Make the deals."

"Wait a minute, kid—"

"Don't be a sucker. You know all the ropes. You've been around this racket long enough. You know the people and what they'll go for."

The man behind the desk held up his hands to stem the flow of words. "Hold it, hold it." When Marlon subsided, Shannon shook his head. "If Cohen ever got wind of it, I'd be out of here on my tail."

"So what? By then we'll be big enough so you can tell him what to do with his job."

"Suppose it don't go big?"

Marlon studied the other man with a new perspective. He had looked up to the plugger as a man with unlimited contacts, unlimited expense account, as a man who had been around, who knew the ropes. Now he saw him as a scared man, scared of losing his job, scared to take a proposition, but more scared not to.

"What are you so scared about, Shannon? I told you it can't miss."

"But if it does—"

"Then don't give up your job until we got it made. Cohen don't have to know." He leaned forward, lowered his voice. "I got this made, Mike, no kidding."

"What's the proposition?"

Marlon took a deep, satisfied breath, leaned back. Much of what he planned for the program required having a man with Shannon's entree and experience working with him. Now that he had better insight into the older man's insecurity, he knew it would end up by Shannon working for him, rather than with him. He liked the prospect better that way.

"How much are you making here?"

"That's nobody's business but mine, kid," the man behind the desk growled around his cigar. "You got a proposition, let's hear it."

Marlon chewed on the cuticle of his thumb. He had been prepared, took for granted it would operate on a fifty-fifty basis. "How about ten per cent of what you book?"

The man behind the desk got to his feet in exasperation. "What do I look like, kid? A damn' fool altogether? Here you're asking me to work with you on a deal that might cost me my job and you think I'd go for it for ten per cent of the take?" He walked around the desk, perched on the corner of it. "I been thinking it over. Maybe you do have an idea, but if I'm going to take a flyer with you, I want to get paid for it."

"What do you think you're worth?"

"Fifty per cent."

Eddie Marlon rose from his chair with a stricken expression. "Fifty per cent?" he shrilled. "I do all the work, I do all the thinking—"

"You came knocking, Eddie. I didn't send for you."

The thin man slumped back into the chair. "I'll go for twenty-five per cent."

Shannon scratched his ear. "Thirty-three."

Marlon considered, nodded. "Thirty-three." They

shook on it. "How soon can you start working on it?"

The older man ran the tips of his fingers along the faint stubble on his chin. "When does the show start?"

"In a couple of weeks."

"I'll have to get going right away making contacts. You can't expect much until the program gets on the air, you know." There was a new wheedling note in his voice that Eddie had heard when the contact man addressed Arnie Cohen. The relationship was established. "People got to start talking about the show before I can really produce." Shannon walked back around the desk, started rooting through the drawer, came up with a pad of yellow sheets. He started scribbling on the top sheet.

Marlon watched for a minute curiously. "Ain't this a funny time to be writing your diary?"

The man behind the desk looked up. "Our contract."

"Contract?"

"Yeah. I want some kind of a guarantee." Shannon straightened up, asked uneasily, "You were figuring on some kind of a contract, weren't you, kid?"

"Why would we need a contract?"

Shannon licked at his lips. "Me, I'm not exactly from Squareville, kid, but you're one character I wouldn't go up against unless I had my legs crossed."

"Okay, if that's the way you feel about it, forget the whole deal." Marlon got up, permitted the other man to wave him back down.

"I don't mean anything by it, kid. It's just that you're plenty sharp and you got more ambition than I got blood corpuscles. That's a bad combination to go up against barehanded."

"No contract. If I can't trust you—"

"You can trust me."

"Okay, then, we don't need any contract." He watched

with satisfaction while the other man tossed the pencil down on the desk, tore the top sheet off the pad, crushed it into a ball.

"No contract, no deal."

Marlon decided to play it hard, shrugged, got up from the chair, and walked to the door. "I'm sorry, Shannon, I thought you were a smart guy. I thought we could do things together."

"I don't mind doing things together, kid. It's just that I want to be sure that it's not you doing it to me all the time." He had a worried frown on his face when Marlon went out and slammed the door behind him.

Eddie Marlon sweated it out for three days awaiting word from Shannon. Nobody was more aware than he of the fact that he needed the plugger badly, if he was to put all his plans into effect. He had almost decided to give in, to call up and say he'd sign the contract, when his telephone rang.

"Eddie? Mike Shannon."

The thin man kept his voice cold, impersonal. "Yeah, Shannon?"

"I want to talk to you, kid. Maybe if I come up there and—"

"What's the point, Shannon? Besides, I'm pretty busy lining up my show. Why don't we just let it lay? I'll be bumping into you around."

There was a note of desperation in the other man's voice. "Now look, kid. I didn't mean anything by what I said. I didn't mean to make you sore. I—"

"I'm not sore, Shannon. Just hurt."

"Okay, I won't take up much of your time. I've been thinking about that deal. Maybe I was wrong. Maybe I—"

"I been thinking it over, too, Mike." Marlon could visualize the older man swabbing at his face as he listened. "I went away overboard. I'm glad we didn't make a deal. Thirty-three per cent! I must've been nuts."

The man on the other end sounded eager. "Look, we won't need a contract. We're good friends and—"

"It's twenty-five per cent now, Shannon. And if it weren't for the fact that I don't want to show in this I wouldn't even agree to that. Why for ten per cent I could get me an agent who—"

There was a deep sigh at the other end of the line. "I'll take it. When can we get together to iron out the details?"

"Why don't you drop up now?"

Marlon dropped the receiver on its hook, grinned his exultation. The Eddie Marlon Show was at last about to be put on the road!

10

Marty Allen flagged Eddie Marlon down in the halls at Republic a week later. There was a jaunty, self-assured smile on the kid's face that was becoming a permanent fixture.

"Hi, kid. How's it going?" He caught him by the arm, pulled him over to the side. "The old man's been having hot flashes worrying about you."

"Nobody has to worry about Eddie Marlon, Allen."

Marty Allen raised his eyebrows. It was the first time the kid had called him Allen. It had started out to be Mr. Allen, had worked its way to a tentative Marty and had settled in that mold. Now it was Allen.

"You know that two-hour behemoth of yours debuts in less than a week and they've only sold five segments. That ain't good, kid."

"How are you doing, Allen?"

Marty Allen nodded. "All right."

"So why are you worryin'? Let me worry about my show. I got it all set up. And if it'll make you feel any better, I'm on my way to talk to Larry Sanders about some spots right now."

"You've got some lined up?"

The fixed smile became broader. "No. I'm just going to set up a priority system. I figure we'll have more than we can handle and I want to make sure we've got a way of not letting anything go to waste." He tapped his knuckles against the bigger man's chest. "Matter of fact, if you're real nice we might push some of the overflow your way."

Allen grinned at him. "That's mighty damn' white of you, kid."

"And another thing, pally. Forget that kid stuff, will you?" He puffed his chest out, squinted a little. "I didn't mind it before, but I don't want any of these other crumbs around here getting familiar."

"What do you want me to call you, master?"

"Eddie will do," the thin man told him coldly. "Look, Allen, I got nothing against you. I think you're a schmoe for passing up all the loot you do pass up. But that's your business. You were okay with me when I was just learning the ropes and so I like you. But get it out of your head that I'm the same little schnook who came looking for a job with his hat in his hand. I learned a lot since then and I'm on my way."

"I hear you've got quite a setup."

"Meaning?"

"Meaning that you don't intend to be a schmoe, too."

Marlon grinned at him again, but the grin didn't reach the eyes. "Take good care of yourself, old boy. I can't stand around and shoot the breeze anymore.

Don't forget to tune in when we get going. There's a lot you can learn."

"I'll bet."

Marty Allen stood in the hallway, watched the pouter-pigeon strut of the thin man as he barreled down the corridor in the direction of the director of spot sales. He was watching the birth of a new era in music and broadcasting and he had only the faintest conception of its implications.

Larry Sanders, charged with spot sales for afternoon broadcasting, was a sad-looking man; the bags under his eyes were like those of a St. Bernard. His nose was large and red, seemed to be constantly running, an illusion he fostered by running the side of his hand under it with disturbing regularity. He looked up as Eddie Marlon stuck his head in the door.

"Sanders? I'm Eddie Marlon."

The sad-eyed man nodded with no show of enthusiasm. "I know." He put aside some papers he had been studying, waved the thin man in.

Marlon walked in, cleared a corner of the desk, perched his hip on it. "I hear you been worrying about me, Sanders."

"Worrying about you? Why should I worry about you? I got enough to do worrying about myself." He opened the top drawer of his desk, pulled out a program sheet. "You got any idea of how much that program of yours stands to cost Republic?" He ran a finger down the sponsor list. "To break even we got to have six segments sponsored. You got five." He looked up. "You know what we had to cancel out to clear that time for you? Eight sponsored segments." He shook his head. "The old man musta gone crazy."

"Crazy like a fox," Marlon told him. He reached over, picked the program sheet from between the other man's fingers. "How about three-minute spots or one-minute spots? You know how many we can sell on each segment? Two or three." He ran his eyes down the list. "You got none."

The sad-eyed man shook his head. "Look, kid. You're not on some 50,000 watter in the hills. This is Republic. We don't sell like a pushcart peddler. We—"

Marlon flipped the sheet back on the desk. "On my show you do." He dug a notebook from his inside pocket, wet a finger, ran through the pages. "I got a list here. People I talked to about the show. I didn't do any selling, you understand. Undignified. But I softened them up." He tore several pages out, dropped them on the desk. "All you've got to do—"

The man behind the desk studied the list with horrified eyes. "This is crap, kid. We never take this kind of advertising on Republic. Cut-rate suits, used cars." He shook his head. "We'll take a bath on the show before we take crap like this."

Marlon reached over, lifted the phone from its cradle, handed it to Sanders. "Call J. K. D." He pressed the instrument into the other man's hand. "Go ahead. Call Dickenson. He'll okay it." When Sanders refused to take the phone, Marlon held it to his own ear.

"Hello. This is Eddie Marlon. Get me John K. Dickenson." He stared at the man behind the desk while he waited. Then said, "J. K.? Eddie Marlon. I'm down at Sanders's office. I have a flock of advertisers for my show and he's raising his nose at them. No, I got them myself. You know, drinking with the right people—" He broke off, nodded. "Okay." He held the receiver out. "He wants to talk to you."

Sanders took the instrument. "Yes, Mr. Dickenson?" He listened respectfully, nodded. "I understand that. But have you seen the type of advertisers? One-minute and two-minute spots. Used-car dealers, cut-rate clothing houses?" The receiver cut him off with a metallic chatter. "All right, Mr. Dickenson. If you say so." He returned the receiver to its hook, pursed his lips, nodded. "All right, Marlon. We'll do it your way."

"Mr. Marlon, Sanders." The thin man jumped from the corner of his desk. "I just ran down these leads to show you how it could be done. I hope I don't have to do the show and sell the time, too, in the future."

"You won't have to. We'll take care of that part of it." He picked up the list and studied it. "There won't be much selling on these. Most of them have been fighting to buy time on this station." He dropped the list into his desk. "You used to work for Marty Allen, didn't you?"

Marlon nodded.

"Then you know that Marty has refused to accept half of these as sponsors."

"I know a lot of things about Allen," the thin man told him without embarrassment. "Mostly, he taught me what not to do." He stared at the man behind the desk for a moment. "What kind of a promotion are you giving me for the opening of the show?"

"Ads in the radio sections of the Sunday papers. Then a follow-up on the radio pages all of next week."

"I haven't seen any of them."

Sanders narrowed his heavy-lidded eyes. "They haven't been approved yet. When they're approved, we'll send you a copy."

"How can they be approved until I see a copy?" The thin man leaned his palms on the desk. "Look, mister. I don't want any trouble with you, but if I got to have it, I know who's walking away from it." He fixed a smile on his lips. "I want to see that promotion and I want to see it before it's placed. Besides, didn't it occur to you that maybe I'd have some ideas on what should go into it?"

"It does now," Sanders conceded.

Marlon dug out the notebook again. "I guess I got to handle that part of it, too." He flipped through the pages. "Here are some of the guests who'll be showing up in person to give the show a big send-off." He rattled off a list of internationally known stars, smirked at the expression of the man in the chair.

"You're guaranteeing those names will appear? On a record show?"

"I don't like the way that sounds, Sanders." Marlon cut him off coldly. "What gave you the idea this was a record show? This is going to be the biggest music-and-talent showcase in radio. And these people are smart enough to get on the bandwagon."

Sanders wiped the dampness from his jowls. "But we got to have a release before we can use their names in ads," he argued. "I don't know who told you they'd show, but if you promise them and can't produce, we're in plenty of trouble."

"Look, mister. You don't know me very long. But when you do, you'll find out that I never promise what I can't produce." He hit the notebook with the back of his hand. "Every one of these will be at the studio next week to launch the show. Now I want that in the advertising."

"Okay, Mr. Marlon. That's the way you want it, that's the way it is. But I take no responsibility for—"

"Who's asking you to? All I'm asking you to do is get on that ball. So far all I've got from your department is arguments. That I can get any place."

"I guess you know what you're doing." Sanders shrugged.

Marlon dropped the notebook in front of him. "Don't

that look like it?" He watched with satisfaction while the ad man ran through the list. "How big was this space you were planning to use to announce the show?"

"Three inches on two columns."

"You better double it. Check J. K. D. for an okay if you think you need one. And another thing—I want some spots on key programs throughout the week selling the Eddie Marlon show."

Sanders started to argue, shrugged. "Okay. I'll take care of it."

11

The debut of the Eddie Marlon show was something short of sensational, but by the time it went off the air all concerned knew they had a hit. It was like Mike Shannon told Marlon in the 500 Bar that night.

"There are some rough edges, kid. But I got to hand it to you. You handled that patter and chatter like an expert. I was watching the guy in the control room—"

"How'd he take it?"

"Big." Shannon grinned. "When the show started I could see he wasn't too sure. Then when the guests started popping in and you started kidding around with them, you shoulda seen his eyes bug."

"How about Arnie Cohen?" Eddie Marlon waved down a waiter, ordered a round of drinks. It almost seemed as though he had grown since the night before. And he had an ease and assurance that only a successful performance can give.

Shannon grinned. "You scored good. If Arnie was a broad, you'd be in. I talked to him on the phone while you were cleaning things up at the studio. He likes."

"Check any of the others?"

"Lonnie Dyers down at Taos, Bob Willis at Conception, all of them. You need talent from now on, you get all you want." He broke off while the waiter slid the water-white Martinis in front of them. "It was a nice job of showcasing the talent, kid. Real big-time."

Marlon sipped at his drink, approved. "I hope they enjoyed it. It's the last time they get it for free."

"Arnie's got a deal for us. Rhythm's getting behind a new Bobby Barris platter. He'll go for a couple of C for a concentrated play over the next ten days. I told him you'd play."

Marlon nodded. "For dough plus."

"Plus what?"

"I got me a real hot idea up there today," the thin man told him. "We got off to a big start. Am I right?"

"Real big."

"Okay, so we can't let it settle down into a rut like Allen's in. We got to keep jabbing the opposition off balance. So that's why I get this idea."

Shannon took a cigar from his pocket, waited patiently.

"We got to get the teen-age crowd lined up solid behind us. Am I right?" Shannon nodded on cue, Marlon continued. "What do kids like best? Something for nothing."

"I never heard of anybody hating that. But what do we give them?"

Marlon took a deep breath, leaned back. "I'm going to take over Madison Square Garden, fill it with kids on the cuff and give them the damnedest in-person show they ever saw."

"You're nuts!" Shannon gasped. "It would cost a mint."

"Not the way I intend to do it. First, I put the arm

on the station and the sponsors to pick up the hot for the Garden. Then, we strong-arm the talent—"

Shannon shook his head. "No dice. Maybe you get a few singers, but no live music."

"Why not?"

"Petrillo. That's why not. That 802 don't play for no."

A deep frown ridged Marlon's forehead. "We can't talk to this Petrillo character?"

"Nobody but God talks to Petrillo." Shannon kept shaking his head. "They even had a tough time getting an okay for a benefit that—"

"That's it."

Shannon looked startled. "What's it?"

"A benefit. We're going to run a benefit, all the funds go to polio or the Heart Fund or cancer. Any one you can line up." He watched the other man's face. "That way we get an okay on the live music."

Shannon pursed his lips. "Could be." He held his glass by the stem, swirled his Martini thoughtfully. "Maybe we could make a tie-in with some soft-drink people or with the Stahl-Meyer outfit and give the kids a coke and a hot dog and—"

Marlon shook his head. "No drinks and dogs on the house. Proceeds go to the charity." He grinned. "After we take our usual cut."

Shannon considered it. "We might be able to swing it, at that."

"Of course we can. The kids will love it, the sponsors get a nice ride, and we pick up some change. We'll make it an annual event and by this time next year we'll have every kid in town eating out of our hands, fighting to get in."

The older man gulped his drink, shook his head. "You go so fast, kid, you scare hell out of me." He waved to the waiter, pointed to his empty glass, held up two fingers. "You really think we can swing it?"

"Why not? We make it big enough and there's not a name performer could afford to stay away from it."

Shannon chewed on his ever-present cigar. "It's a big order."

"We're shooting for big stakes." Marlon eyed the unlighted cigar in the other man's mouth with distaste. "Don't you ever set fire to those things?"

"No. Smoking's bad for my stomach." Shannon's mind was racing miles away. The stunt would be colossal—either a colossal success or a colossal flop. It would depend on how hard they could shake the A and R men at the various companies, how far the publicity departments of the big movie outfits would go along. The more he thought about it, the more he was inclined to agree that no major artist could refuse to take part. "When would you hold this?"

"Three months from now. From now until then, we just plug for it. Word about a thing like that gets around."

"What will Dickenson and the brass at the station say about it?"

Marlon shrugged. "What *can* they say? It's a promotion, isn't it? It's going to do the station as much good as it will me." He drained his glass, set it down. "If we swing this one, Mike, we've got a waiting list of sponsors as long as your arm fighting to get on the bandwagon."

Shannon nodded. "And there's not a publisher or record outfit in the business that won't come through without a murmur," he admitted. "What's the first step?"

"We sit back for a day or two and see how the show was received."

The waiter came, deposited two fresh Martinis,

picked up the empty glasses, shuffled back toward the bar.

"Okay, so on that one we're playing with marked cards. You know they're going to love it. What next?"

"Then I sit down with John K. Dickenson. I lay out the blueprint and I offer to let him in on it. He don't want it, and I'll threaten to take it to somebody else." He sipped his drink. "He didn't figure I could carry off a show like today. Now he's not too sure I can't do anything I say I can do." He was beginning to feel just a little high, a combination of success and Martinis. "And I'm not so sure I can't, either."

John K. Dickenson had listened to the opening of the Eddie Marlon show in his private office. As the show moved smoothly from segment to segment, most of his misgivings disappeared. He checked off in the ads the names of celebrities whose presence had been promised, breathed a sigh of relief when the last name had been reached. Not a single name had failed to make an appearance! When the show was over he knew that Republic had a real property on its hands. He pressed the button on the side of his desk that turned the radio on and off, lifted his receiver.

"Betty," he told the cool blonde in the outer office. "Tell Larry Sanders I want to see him right away." He was standing at the window, staring down onto Madison Avenue many stories below when the sad-eyed man shuffled into his office. Dickenson swung around.

"What about it, Larry?"

"A winner, Mr. Dickenson. Don't ask me how or why. But the little bastard's got a winner." He walked over to one of the leather chairs, dropped into it. "He wasn't through the second segment before the damn' phone started to ring." He shook his head as though he couldn't believe his own words. "You know we actually had to turn down fifteen-minute sponsors. Just because we're loaded with all those cheap suits and second-hand cars and—"

Dickenson walked back to his chair, dropped into it. "Don't worry about that. Sometimes it does them good to turn them down. Makes them more anxious." He swung his chair around, slid open a panel in the bar cabinet. "Use a drink, Larry?"

The ad man nodded. "Trouble is, by the time the cheap stuff's time has been used up, these other deals will be out of heat." He watched while the white-haired man took out a bottle, two glasses and some ice.

"You don't think he can keep it up?"

Sanders shrugged. "Let's face it. Anybody can set a show on fire if he's got a million dollars' worth of big-name talent—"

"On the cuff," Dickenson reminded him. He dropped two ice cubes into each glass, covered them with whisky, pushed one across the desk.

"On the cuff, or not on the cuff. Fact is he had more big names on that show of his today than the old Rudy Vallee show used to have in a month." He sipped at his drink, approved, settled back with a sigh. "What happens when there's only him, a few platters and a turntable?"

"I don't know. I thought the kid's chatter was pretty interesting. Fast, brash, gagged up."

Sanders dabbed at the discolored tip of his nose, nodded. "He's pretty good, I'll admit that. But he's got to have a gimmick to last."

"Why?"

"Today he's a novelty. Today all the housewives stop listening to their favorite soap operas to tune in on these big names. Maybe tomorrow some of that audience will stick. But, slowly but surely, they're going to drift back to their soaps. It's bound to happen."

"Unless he has a gimmick?"

"Unless he has a gimmick. But what kind of a gimmick he could have on a show like that I don't know." He shook his head sadly. "I wish those other segments were open. That way we could tie some new sponsors up for at least thirteen weeks and get off the hook before he does fold."

Dickenson chewed on his lower lip thoughtfully. "I felt the same way you did, Larry. But somehow, I've got faith in that kid's dogged determination. If it's a gimmick he needs, I've got the feeling he'll come up with one."

The sad-eyed man groaned. "I got the same feeling, chief, and I'm not sure I like the feeling."

"You're planning a follow-up on the promotion on today's show?"

"All the columnists have been contacted. We should get some real raves on it. Like I said, it's not now I'm worried about. It's in a couple of months, when he's just another platter spinner making with the words and trying to kid the sponsor without stepping on his toes."

"Maybe you're right. But in the meantime, Larry, let's stay on top of it. Sell time contingent on cancellation of some of the spots we now have. Tie it up as tight as you can."

Sanders swallowed his drink, nodded. "Will do, chief." He set his glass on the corner of the desk. "Not that there'll be anything for us to do. That little eager beaver is probably out right now selling time and contacting the columnists. It's not that he doesn't think anybody else can do anything, he just doesn't think they can do it as good."

12

The Eddie Marlon Music Marathon in Madison Square Garden was a ten-day sensation in the trade. Not every big star in New York turned out for it, but enough did to keep the record-breaking throng in delirium. Lines of teen-agers besieged the Garden hours before the doors were scheduled to be opened. For three months Eddie Marlon had plugged the show, had promised there would be no entrance fee and that the lucky guests of his program would enjoy hours on end of music from top bands, and songs from top music personalities. By the time the show was scheduled to start, the Garden was packed and a mob of youngsters was still fighting to get in.

In the center of the floor, where the fight ring is usually erected, a huge platform had been built. On it stood a small bandstand, a piano, and a desk. The spotlights from the ceiling were focused on the desk, other floods lighted the bandstand.

At exactly eight, Eddie Marlon took his place at the desk. A mike setup had been arranged for him there, his papers were carefully piled in the center of the desk. A bevy of showgirls, on loan from the biggest night clubs, were scurrying around, acting as messengers.

When the small figure appeared on the stage and took its place at the desk, a roar went up that shook the walls of the Garden. He looked around at the sea of faces that seemed to extend to infinity, held his hands over his head in the traditional gesture of the successful boxer. This brought on another roar.

Mike Shannon had done a herculean job of lining

up talent. Not only had he put the arm on the A and R man of his company, but of every company in the business. He had used his contacts among the bandsmen and their vocalists, among the producers of the tab musicals that were the rage of the night clubs that season, the top vocalists themselves. He had scored more often than he had missed. And as he stood at the entrance to the stage, he knew that those who had refused the urgent invitation to "show up and say hello" might well regret it.

He knew when he had tied up with Eddie Marlon that the kid was a dynamo, destined to go places—on sheer nerve if not talent. He had stepped into a field where muscle and nerve were the determining factor. The turnout here tonight was proof enough of the kid's inborn appreciation of the larceny in every soul.

To be a success in the field the thin man had picked out for himself, Eddie Marlon was ideally equipped. It was no spot for anybody fastidious or wishy-washy like Marty Allen. It was a job for a man who knew what he wanted and was determined to get what he wanted without being disturbed or concerned for the feelings of those he had to step on to get it.

Shannon was aware that tonight Eddie Marlon had started his blacklist. Tonight the names of those who did not appear on the program would be given special prominence in his mind. It would be a matter of personal pride to chastise those who saw in him someone so unimportant that his invitation could be ignored. He was in a spot where he must be realistic. Either they were with him or against him, and he was the type to believe that if they thought a setback or discouragement couldn't hurt him—well, a more serious setback shouldn't make much difference to them. And he was in a position to help foment the setback.

Even in the midst of the tremendous success of his Music Marathon, Eddie Marlon was brooding. Some of the stars who had failed to make an appearance hedged the possibility of its success with a telegram of regrets and good wishes. Only Tony DeSales, a fast-rising young crooner, had taken the time to say what he really thought.

YOUR INVITATION TO APPEAR GRATIS AT A SELF-GLORIFYING MARATHON IS GRATE-FULLY DECLINED. I GET PAID FOR WHAT I DO AND ANYTHING YOU GET FOR NOTHING IS WORTH THAT. ANY TIME YOU FEEL YOU WANT TO PAY MY RATES, CONTACT MY MANAGER. TONY DESALES.

That night a feud was born that was destined to rock Music Row. But all Eddie Marlon could think of when he received the telegram was how to hit back, and to hit back hard enough to make a horrible ex-ample of Tony DeSales.

All through the evening, as he introduced act after act, each with a little anecdote, some background, and a heavy plug, he brooded.

The Music Marathon roared to a tremendous clos-ing at 1 a.m. having racked up the biggest aggregation of talent ever to have appeared in New York for what the trade called "for no." As the singing, stamping teenagers poured out all the exits into the streets and avenue, Eddie Marlon permitted Mike Shannon to pump his arm.

"You did it, kid. You really did it," Shannon roared.

"Thanks, Mike. Got a drink on you? My throat feels like beefsteak." He waited while Shannon shouldered his way through a crowd surrounding the bar Leo

Lindy had set up for the talent.

When Shannon came back with a large Scotch and soda, he told Marlon. "Nobody could have figured you'd pull it off. Nobody. It was a sensation. Winchell came back to have a look around, Sullivan was out front. You really hit the jackpot, kid."

Marlon pulled the crumpled telegram from DeSales from his jacket pocket. "You see this?"

Shannon read through it, shrugged. "So what? So a hundred guys ten times bigger showed, didn't they?"

"I'm going after him, Mike." Eddie took a deep swallow from his glass, coughed. "I'm going after the little bastard and take him apart."

"Now what the hell are you going to do that for?"

"Because once one of these crumbs thinks he can get away with stiffing us, the rest will try it."

Shannon shook his head violently. "Let well enough alone. Why let him know he even bothers you? You see that mob out there tonight, kid? Well, so did your sponsors. So did the station people. They never saw anything like it in their lives. You got it made, kid."

"I'm gonna cut the bastard down to size," Marlon brooded.

Shannon started to argue, shrugged. "You're all keyed up. It was one helluva show you put on there. One helluva show. How about it? We go out, get us a couple of broads, get rid of some of that pressure?"

Marlon drained the glass, handed it back. "Got anything special in mind?"

"How about Dotty and Jackie? You seemed to go for Dotty."

"A lay." Marlon shrugged. "And that friend of hers? What's her name?"

"Jackie."

"She drives me crazy with that damn' yatta-yatta."

"You think I take her out because I like her conversation?" Shannon was miffed. "Okay, so you name the broads. Who'd you like—?" He named a well-stacked blonde movie star.

"Get me that and I'll take it."

"So will a million other guys. So you can't have that, why don't you take what you can get?"

"Okay. If you promise to keep that broad of yours quiet. Tonight I got all the noise and chatter I can take." He reread the telegram from DeSales. "The dirty bastard!"

The girls danced in the line at Harry and Charley's, a boisterous little boîte on West 52nd Street. When Eddie Marlon and Mike Shannon walked in, the floor show was on, with Harry Lewis singing the sad lament of the girl who went up the mountain.

Marlon elected to sit at the bar and reread for the hundredth time the saucy cartoons that lined the room. Shannon disappeared for a moment after a whispered apology. He had barely returned to perch on the barstool at Eddie's side when on the floor Harry Lewis held his arms up to cut off the band.

"Just a minute, ladies and gentlemen. Someone just came in I want you to meet. Eddie Marlon, the world's greatest disc jockey. Maybe some of you were fortunate enough to be at the Garden tonight when every top star of stage, screen, and radio—including yours truly—turned out to pay tribute to him and his great radio show." He pointed to where Marlon sat and a beam of light picked him out. "Take a bow, Eddie. Take a dozen of them."

The applause, always triggered by Harry Lewis's pointing finger, exploded at them.

From his barstool Eddie Marlon waved to the performers on the floor, grasped his hands over his head.

When the spotlight returned to the doings on the small raised stage, Marlon jabbed Mike Shannon with his elbow. "You know, I'm beginning to think that maybe you're worth the money you hijacked out of me."

"Yeah. If it ever starts coming."

After the show the chorus girls came out from backstage, gravitated toward the various tables. Two of them, one small, dark, and vivacious, the other tall and chestnut-haired, headed for the bar.

Dotty, the small brunette, scrambled up onto the stool alongside Eddie Marlon. "I hear you killed them tonight, honey." She held smeary lips up to be kissed. "The kids backstage were all talking about you."

"You should've been there," Shannon said. "Tonight he's the biggest thing in radio." He turned to Jackie. "What's the matter with you? You can't say hello?"

"Complain, complain, complain. That's all you ever do. First you tell me to keep my mouth shut. That this character—"

Shannon hit his brow with the flat of his hand.

"What a dumb broad! Look, you can say hello. You can say good-by, you can say yes. Outside of that, keep your mouth shut."

Marlon ignored her, turned to the little brunette. "You got to do the three o'clock show?"

She shook her head. "Harry let us off. What've you got in mind?"

"A little relaxation. How about Pietro's?"

"Sounds okay to me," Shannon said and nodded. He looked to the girls. Jackie shrugged, pulled a pocket mirror from her bag, smoothed the heavy smear on her lips with the ball of her little finger. Dotty, he knew, would go for anything Eddie suggested.

In the cab on the way from Harry and Charley's to

Pietro's, Eddie Marlon was unusually quiet. He didn't even indulge in the usual grab-and-squeeze techniques that characterized his taxicab trips. Even Jackie noticed it.

"What's with the genius?" she wanted to know.

"Look, the guy's had a bad night."

Jackie giggled. "He don't even know what a bad night is. He should have to put up with you after you've had a few and you want—"

"Will you shut up?" Shannon growled.

Dotty snuggled closer to Marlon who sat, chin in hand, looking out the cab window. "Tired, honey? Maybe you'd prefer to go home?"

"No. I want to see if any of the gang's at Pietro's." He turned, patted the girl's knee. "I feel okay."

"But something is bothering you."

"Yeah. But nothing I can't handle in my own way."

"What is it?" Dotty persisted.

"Oh, that creep groaner, DeSales. The bum didn't show tonight."

Dotty frowned. "So what? Everybody else did from what I hear."

"That's what I keep trying to tell him," Shannon grunted. "It was one helluva turnout. So one groaner don't make it. Does that mean—"

"It's the principle of the thing," Marlon grunted. "He gets away with it, the rest of them are gonna start to feel they can push me around."

"No more, kid," Shannon assured him. "After what you pulled tonight, nobody pushes. They see a solid gang of kids like that behind you, they know you got some weight to throw around."

"How many were there?" Dotty wanted to know.

"Who knows? Thousands. The Garden was jam-packed. Solid," Shannon enthused. "You shoulda seen

Winchell's eyes pop when he takes a look around. There ain't an empty seat in the house."

"The price was right," Jackie snorted.

"I thought you were going to make that broad button her lip," Marlon growled. "I want funny sayings, I'll turn on Jack Benny."

"She don't mean nothing," Shannon said.

"She don't say nothing, either. But those noises that come out of her annoy me."

He let Shannon get the cab bill when they got to Pietro's. He caught Dotty by the arm, walked her across the sidewalk.

Pietro's is a side street example of what Hollywood would have the world believe a New York restaurant is like: dim lights, red-checked table cloths, a string ensemble and tables dotted with familiar, famous faces. Here was the place where Radio Row liked to foregather to lick its wounds, brag about its successes and minimize its failures.

The minute they walked in, it was obvious that Eddie Marlon had no reason to seek Pietro's to minimize any failures. Familiar faces who were little more than familiar faces waved to him as he came in. From a back table, Marty Allen waved for them to come over.

He was sitting with a tall redhead with milky skin. He had been drinking heavily, but he wasn't drunk. He pushed himself to his feet as Eddie Marlon came to the table.

"Nice work, kid." With raised hand, he cut himself off. "Mr. Marlon, that is." He turned to the woman at his table. "You never met my wife, did you, Mr. Marlon?"

"Cut it out, Marty. You don't have to kid me. So I got lucky."

Allen staggered just the slightest bit. "I can't be

drunk. Did I detect humility? No. Anyway, kid, congratulations."

"You'd better sit down, Marty." His redheaded wife caught his hand, pulled him back into his seat. "I was at the Garden tonight, Mr. Marlon. Your show was sensational."

"Thanks." He nodded briefly, took Dotty by the arm, walked back to meet Shannon and Jackie. "The bum. The no-good, drunken bum," he growled under his breath. "He's jealous. That's what he is."

"Sure, honey," Dotty consoled him. "That's all he is. Jealous."

13

The following morning, Eddie Marlon awakened with sticky eyes, a throbbing headache and a mouth full of cotton. He groaned softly, tried to turn over, only to collide with another body. He managed to get his eyes open wide enough to identify Dotty, lying on her back, her mouth slightly open, her black hair scattered over the pillow.

He drew back the covers, swung his feet out, sat on the side of the bed raking his fingers through his hair. He tried to determine at what point of the night before he lost track of the proceedings, could remember vaguely leaving Pietro's for a bottle club Shannon knew in the Sixties. From there, the events of the night became very vague.

He got up, stumbled toward the small kitchenette. He spilled some tomato juice into a glass, drank it. It was wet and cold. He finished the waking up process by lurching into the bathroom where he splashed cold water onto his face.

On the bed, the girl was mumbling her way to consciousness. After a moment she sat up, the covers fell to her waist, baring small breasts. She looked around, as though orienting herself to her surroundings; her eyes finally came to rest on Marlon coming out of the bathroom.

She worked on a tentative smile. "Hello."

"What time's it on that clock?" he wanted to know.

"Ten."

He shook his head, placed his hand across his eyes. "We sure tied one on last night. What time did we get back here?"

"About six." She watched him make his way across the room. "You all right?"

He sat on the edge of the bed. "I've felt better and thought I was going to die."

"Anything in the columns?"

He wrinkled his brow in an attempt to understand what she had said. "Columns?"

"About the Marathon last night."

"Forgot all about it. Look, baby, do me a favor. Get the papers. They're outside the door."

He watched while she slipped out of bed, crossed the floor naked. For a small girl, her hips slipped up and down with real rhythm. She opened the door a crack, reached through, brought in a small pile of newspapers. She recrossed the room, dropped them on the bed beside him, fingered through the *Mirror*. She read for a minute, then said, "Listen to this. Nick Kenny said it was the biggest collection of top-flight talent ever assembled." She read a few more lines. "He calls you the Pied Piper of Pop Music."

Marlon was busy reading Ed Sullivan's "Little Old New York." The frown had drained from his face. "Sullivan says if this is an annual event it could get as big as the Harvest Moon Ball. Wonders why nobody else ever thought of doing it."

"Winchell calls you Mister Big of Music. Says after this you can make them or break them, and—"

Marlon looked up, grabbed for the paper. "Let me see that." He read and reread the three lines in Winchell's column. "We're in, baby, we're in. From here on in, they either ride along with us, or they're strictly in Nowhereville."

After breakfast he dropped Dotty at a small rooming house where she shared quarters with Jackie. He kept the cab, didn't get out at her place, headed uptown to the Republic executive offices.

Marty Allen was standing in the corridor on the fifteenth floor, chinning with one of the engineers where the elevator deposited Eddie Marlon. He grinned as the small man came abreast.

"I understand I saw you last night, kid. If I forgot to tell you, you had a damn' good show."

"You told me," Marlon grunted.

"What's the matter? You don't sound your usual eager self this morning."

"Why shouldn't I be? You see Winchell, Sullivan or Nick Kenny this morning?"

Allen grinned. "I'm lucky I can open my eyes, let alone read any columns. Besides, I don't have to read any columns to know you're a genius."

"Look, Allen, I got no sense of humor this early in the morning. I don't like getting ribbed." He pushed past, headed for the small office he had wangled as his own.

Shannon was sitting in the chair behind the desk when Marlon walked in. The ex-plugger looked as though the evening had been a big one. The ever-present cigar drooped at half-mast, the eyes were barely visible above the discolored sacs.

"I been ringing your pad," he greeted Marlon. "Thought you might have overslept." He indicated a typewritten slip on the desk. "Here are the contracts to handle. Two plays a day on the Conception disc. That's for two and a half. Arnie wants an even heavier play than we've been giving that new Dinah Reed side. She'll be up for the second segment for an interview."

"What's he going for?"

"Two fifty and a personal appearance. That ain't bad."

Marlon nodded. "Okay." He ran his eye down the list of paid plugs. "We ought to start doing better than this. Right?"

Shannon shrugged. "We're doing all right for the time we've been on." He took the cigar from his mouth, tossed it at the wastebasket. "We—"

"Get that thing out of there," Marlon growled. He waited while Shannon dug the cigar from the basket, walked to the window and threw it out. "Stinks the whole place out."

"You know, I been thinking. Maybe a year's too long to wait for another Marathon. We can't let it cool down."

"We won't. I got an idea how to handle that."

"What?"

Marlon dropped into his chair, hooked his heels on the edge of the desk. "We're going to do a one-a-week personal appearance. Do the show from a school. On Saturdays, maybe."

"All live, you mean?"

"No. We spin some discs, we talk with some of the kids, we bring in some live talent. A real ball."

Shannon looked at him with renewed respect. "Say,

that ain't bad."

"Bad? It's damn' good. Like that, we got the schools behind us, we get a closer hold on the kids. We maybe arrange to win us some kind of an award from the Mayor or the Governor or somebody—"

"For what?"

"For helpin' fight juvenile delinquency, that's for what. We're teachin' these kids to love music, we're keepin' them off the streets. Damn it. We're doin' a helluva job."

"It's going to cost some dough."

"For what?"

"For a remote. You got to move equipment, tables, everything to the school. Right? Who pays?"

Marlon shrugged. "Who cares? The sponsors, the station. It's public-service stuff, isn't it?"

"I like it," Shannon admitted cautiously. "I don't think we'll have any trouble with the talent."

"That's your department. You got a couple of weeks to kick it around. There's no hurry about it. We can ride for a while on the Marathon. Then when that starts to cool off, we spring the school concerts on them. You like?"

Shannon bobbed his head. "I like."

"Okay. Then you take it from there. Right?"

"Right."

Marlon picked up the list of records scheduled for the afternoon show. His eyes searched through the titles. "We got any DeSales?"

Shannon shook his head. "I figured from now on he's stiffed."

"Schedule two of his new ones." He scowled at the paper. "One to go just before the 3:30 news, the other before the 4:30 news."

"I don't get it. I thought you had the knife out for

him."

Marlon grinned at him. "See what a narrow-minded character you are. Just because the guy can't get to my show, you think I'm mad?" He watched Shannon heading for the record library, shaking his head.

When the door had closed behind the ex-plugger, Marlon picked up the phone. "Who's the engineer on my show today? This is Marlon." He waited until he got the information. "Can you reach him any place? Try Murph's. He usually hits there just before show-time." He tapped his fingers on the edge of the desk, waited while the operator tried to locate the engineer. "I'm sorry, Mr. Marlon, I can't seem to reach him."

"Okay. Keep trying. Tell him I want him to check with me before the show goes on the air. Got that? He's to check with me before the show goes on the air. I don't want any slip-up."

"Yes, sir. I'll tell him."

He had barely replaced the receiver on its hook when the phone buzzed.

"Mr. Marlon?" It was the cool voice of the blonde in John K. Dickenson's office.

"Marlon speaking."

"Mr. Dickenson would like to speak to you. By the way, I was at your show last night. I thought it was sensational."

"If I'd known you liked that kind of thing, you could have come with me."

"Thanks very much, but I had an escort." The icy note was back. There was a click, then John K. Dickenson's voice filled the receiver. "Eddie? This is J. K. My boy, you were sensational last night. Have you seen the papers?"

"I didn't have to see the papers, J. K. I was there, re-member?"

Dickenson laughed heartily. "You've certainly proved your point, Eddie. Larry Sanders tells me he's jammed with requests for time on your show. We can't begin to handle all of them."

"That's simple. Give me another hour."

Dickenson's laughter was a little strained this time. "I'd like to. I really would. But I'm not so sure that—"

"Suit yourself, J. K. If you want me to tackle another hour, I'll be glad to. This is just the beginning. I've got a couple of other stunts."

"Really?" Dickenson's voice had a cautious note. "Such as?"

"I'm tying in with the high schools to fight juvenile delinquency."

"Good, good." The heartiness was back.

"We're going to remote our show every Saturday from a different high school. The kids will be encouraged to come, discuss music, meet their favorite stars. That kind of thing. What do you think?"

There was a brief pause. "I think it sounds great. But what makes you think you can deliver these stars week after week?"

"That's my part, J. K. Am I right?"

"Sure, sure."

"Your part will be to get the turntables and the remote set up for me. I figure we might cop a public-service award for the station."

"I see." Dickenson's voice sounded as though he was thinking deeply. "It might be expensive, but I really think you've got something there, Eddie. I'll go for it. Come in and talk to me about it when you've got it lined up."

"I'll do that, J. K. Thanks for calling." He tossed the receiver back on its hook, stared at it for a moment, then snapped his fingers. "In the palm of my hand."

He was still smiling when Shannon walked back into the room.

"That smile," Mike grunted. "Somebody just got had. I hope it wasn't me."

"Dickenson. He just called to congratulate me on last night's show and I put the arm on him for an extra hour."

"Did he go for it?"

Marlon shook his head. "Not yet. But I figured he wouldn't want to turn me down on two things the same day, so then I hit him with the school concert deal."

"Don't tell me—"

"Hook, line, and sinker. What's more, he didn't struggle. He likes the idea!"

"You didn't just step in it, buster, you've been rolling in it."

The phone on the desk buzzed. Eddie Marlon grabbed it. "Who?" He waited a minute, frowned. "Oh, yeah," the frown cleared. "Sorry, Joe, I didn't recognize the name. Look, there's something I want you to take care of for me from now on. I'm scheduling a Tony De-Sales record just before the 3:30 news and again just before the 4:30 news." He looked up at Shannon and grinned. "I want you to make real sure you louse them up, but good."

The metallic chatter of the voice on the other end came through the receiver.

"I know, I know. I don't care how you do it. The more he sounds like Donald Duck, the better." He nodded at something the man at the other end had to say, then hung up.

"Any questions?" he asked Shannon.

The ex-plugger groaned and sat down hard. "Here's where the merry-go-round really starts to spin!"

14

By the time the Eddie Marlon show had celebrated its first birthday, there was no doubt in the minds along Radio Row that a new, potent force had come on the local scene. The impact of the show on the teen-agers was evident even to his least enthusiastic rooter, and the promised priority list on sponsors was now a reality instead of a boast.

A few days after his first anniversary, Eddie Marlon strolled into John K. Dickenson's office. The blonde in the outer office eyed him with no show of enthusiasm.

"J. K. in?"

"I'll see."

Marlon grinned at her. "What are you giving me, you'll see? He goes in through that door and comes out through that door. So, is he in or out?"

"He's in," the blonde conceded. "But I'll have to announce you."

"Don't bother. He's always glad to see me." The thin man walked to the door, pushed it open. Dickenson looked up from a stack of papers on his desk, frowned his disapproval. The blonde stood behind Marlon in the doorway. "I'm sorry, Mr. Dickenson. Mr. Marlon wouldn't let me announce him."

Dickenson nodded to the girl, turned over the papers he had been reading. "That's all right." He nodded to Marlon. "Come in, Marlon."

Marlon grinned at the blonde, shut the door behind him. "I've been wanting to talk to you, J. K. A couple of things have come up and I figure it's about time we got them cleared away."

Dickenson watched the disc jockey as he crossed the

floor and dropped into a leather overstuffed chair. "I guess you forgot we had a deal."

"I don't think so," Dickenson told him evenly. "I believe we've been living up to our end?"

Marlon shrugged. "It shouldn't have been hard. Not with all the money I've been bringing into the station." He stuck a cigarette in the corner of his mouth. "Or hadn't you noticed?"

The station president nodded. "We're very satisfied. The Eddie Marlon Show is all you said it would be." He reached across the desk, picked a cigar from the humidor, started to remove it from its metal container.

The man across the desk from him touched a match to his cigarette, took a deep drag. "Too bad I can't say the same."

"I had no idea you were dissatisfied."

"We have a lot more sponsors than we can handle. That means I'm passing up a lot of loot I should be getting. Am I right?"

Dickenson considered the statement judicially, nodded. "You could put it that way. But from our point of view, I'd rather you had more prospective sponsors than you can handle than not enough."

Marlon studied the lighted end of his cigarette. "I think I'm going to need more time." He rolled his eyes upward. "Say about three hours in the morning."

The white-haired man stopped with the unlighted cigar halfway to his lips. "Three hours in the morning?"

"Yeah."

Dickenson shook his head. "We don't have that kind of time available, Eddie. Marty Allen goes off the air at nine, and—" He broke off, stared at the other man.

Marlon stuck the cigarette between his lips, inhaled a mouthful of smoke, blew it at the ceiling.

"Wait a minute. You're not suggesting that we turn Marty Allen's time over to you, are you?"

The eyes rolled down from the ceiling. "Why not? We've got enough sponsors waiting in line to make it worthwhile."

"Just a minute, Marlon. We're satisfied with Marty Allen, and—"

The man in the leather chair shrugged. "Okay, if that's the way you want it. Maybe you won't be after I'm done bucking him."

"What do you mean?"

"I was just trying to be loyal to you, J. K. After all, you did give me my first break—"

"Never mind that. What do you mean by bucking him?"

"We had a one-year deal. Remember?"

Dickenson stuck the cigar between his teeth, chewed on it. "Go on."

"I got a proposition from Si Hewitt over at Consolidated Broadcasting. He wants me to write my own ticket for time." He reached over, tapped the ash from the end of his cigarette. "A morning and an afternoon show." He leaned back, returned the cigarette to his lips. "Naturally before I considered it, I contacted most of my sponsors."

"Naturally," Dickenson grunted dryly.

"They'll string along with me any place I go." He dug into his pocket, brought out a legal-sized piece of paper. "Several months ago I took the time to copyright the name and idea of the Music Marathon and the School Concerts. As long as you're not interested, I'll take the whole shooting match over to Consolidated."

"Wait a minute," Dickenson growled. He reached for his phone. "Get me Larry Sanders down in spot sales."

He kept his eyes on the little man in the chair while he waited. "Larry? John K. Dickenson. I want to ask you something. In the event Eddie Marlon left the station, how much of his business do you think he could take with him?" A frown furrowed his forehead at the answer, he sank his teeth into his cigar. "That much, eh?" He nodded curtly. "Okay, thanks." He slammed the receiver back on its hook. "Larry seems to agree with you that you can take a pretty good share of your business with you."

Marlon shrugged. "You don't think I'd say so if I couldn't?" He hooked one leg over the arm of the chair, settled back. "I sold most of this business personally and I've kept everyone else away from it. It goes with me."

"I don't suppose it would do any good to remind you that Marty Allen has been a real friend to you."

"You were right the first time. It wouldn't do any good."

Dickenson nodded grimly. "That's what I thought." He picked up a lighter from the desk, snapped it into flame, touched it to the cigar. "Okay, I'll listen."

Marlon nodded. "You mean you have a choice?"

Marty Allen heard about it that afternoon over cocktails at Pietro's. Ann was in for the afternoon to do some shopping and John K. Dickenson had invited her to join him and Marty for a drink.

The white-haired man sat moodily at the bar, toying with his drink, as though having difficulty getting started. "Marty, aren't you getting a little tired of getting up in the middle of the night?" he asked finally.

Marty pursed his lips, shook his head. "Not particularly. After all these years I'm getting pretty attached to that program."

Dickenson took a deep swallow from his glass. "Marty, I'm over a barrel. I hope you'll understand my position—"

"Marlon?" Allen asked softly.

The white-haired man nodded miserably. "Marlon."

"What are you two talking about?" Ann wanted to know. "It sounds like one of those routines the Two Black Crows used to do."

"Wait a minute, honey." Allen didn't take his eyes off his boss's face. "He wants my time, J. K.?"

Dickenson nodded.

"But why?" Ann wanted to know. "He already has practically the entire afternoon schedule." She looked from her husband to Dickenson and back.

"He wants to be Mister Big in this racket, honey," Allen told her. He continued to study Dickenson's face. "What'd you tell him?"

The white-haired man turned to meet Allen's eyes. "He's had an offer from Consolidated. They want him for as many hours a day as he'll take. If I let him go over there, he'll take most of his billing with him—"

"You're not considering letting Marty go? After all these years?"

Dickenson looked uncomfortable. "Not letting him go, Ann. There's always a spot for Marty at Republic."

"But you are going to turn my time over to Marlon?"

Dickenson shrugged. "I have no choice, Marty. You can understand my position. I have no choice."

Allen nodded. "Sure, I understand your position." He caught Ann by the arm. "Come on, honey, all of a sudden I need some air."

The white-haired man sighed. "Marty, don't be crazy. I know what you're thinking. You're figuring on going over to Consolidated and signing on there for a show to buck Marlon."

"So?"

"Look, pal, we've been friends for too many years for me to let you sucker yourself like that. You can't buck the little rat, Marty, it just can't be done."

"Well, I'm going to give it the old college try."

The redhead shook her head. "John's right, Marty. You don't know how to play dirty enough to play in his league."

Allen raised his eyebrows. "You too?"

"I'm with you, honey, you know that," Ann told him. "But this is a tough world we live in. Marlon knows all the dirty punches and all the spots to stick the knife. You think the music people would string along with you in preference to him?"

"I've always given them a fair shake."

Dickenson shook his head sadly. "But he's the boy who sells the platters for them. He's the boy who makes or breaks a disc." He warded off an interruption with upraised hands. "I know he shakes them for it, but they expect it. That's the kind of operation they understand."

Allen slid back onto the barstool. "You really believe that, J. K.?"

"Of course. You think this pay-off business is new? The music publishers have been doing it since before God. They built themselves a Frankenstein's monster with their pluggers and their pay-offs and now they're crying because it's got bigger than they are."

"Funny thing is, I gave the little bastard his start." Allen grinned wryly. "When I think of all the breath I wasted explaining to him the importance of being ethical." He shook his head. "And all the time the son-ofabitch was laughing at me under his breath."

"That's the way it goes sometimes," Dickenson said. "There's no sense in bucking your head against the wall if you don't stand a chance of winning, is there?"

"I guess not." Allen's shoulders slumped. He watched gratefully while the bartender slid a fresh drink in front of him. "Thanks, Tony."

The man behind the bar winked understandingly.

"Well, what do I do for Republic if I lose my time? Become vice-president in charge of Eddie Marlon, God forbid?"

"You name the spot, Marty."

Allen shook his head. "There's nothing else I can do. I was never cut out for a desk job, J. K. I'm strictly an ex-columnist and ex-disc jockey and that's all I'll ever be."

"I have an idea, John," Ann put in quietly. "You know there's nobody in the business who knows as many people in the trade or is as highly thought of as Marty."

Dickenson nodded.

"A very costly reputation, apparently," Allen grunted. "From what I gather it's a lot more profitable to be a fourteen-carat bastard."

"Why don't you put Marty in charge of trade relations where his contacts with the music people and the columnists and the newspapermen will pay off for both of you?"

The white-haired man considered it, nodded. "Sounds good to me, Marty. How about you?"

"Do you think Eddie Marlon will approve?"

"Cut it out, Marty," Ann scolded. "You know the spot John's in. He's not doing this because he likes it."

Allen nodded. "Okay, so I'm acting like a spoiled brat. Sure, J. K. If you think I can do the job, you've just got yourself a boy."

"And with you working sensible hours like other people, it looks like I've got myself a man," Ann grinned. "A full-time man."

15

For the next few weeks, Eddie Marlon and Mike Shannon were kept busy with the details on the new morning show and a special School Concert. With the help of Republic's press department, the School Concerts got a big send-off in the press and the columns.

The day before the special concert, Shannon came in waving a copy of *Radio Confidential*. He grinned at Marlon. "You're really in, Eddie. Did you see what Ted Brand says about you in his column this morning? He says—"

"I didn't see it, but if the bastard didn't call me the Golden Boy of Radio, I went for a hundred and a half for nothing."

"You got your money's worth," Shannon said, folded the paper, and dropped it on the desk. "Engineering department got the bugs worked out for the remote?"

"They've been bitching like hell, but I think they've got it licked." Marlon smoothed the long hair over his ears with the flat of his hand. "You know, there ought to be an angle in these School Concerts."

"It mightn't be too smart, kid. We're doing all right."

"What's all right? How high is up?" Marlon slapped the top of his desk with the flat of his hand. "We're riding a big deal, buster, and we got to get as much mileage out of it as we can before it blows up."

Shannon shook his head. "This one isn't a short run, Eddie. You really started something. I been listening in on some of the A and R men. They don't know from nothing but radio plugs these days."

Marlon grinned. "No kiddin'?"

"The kids are off on a big-time disc kick. Platters

are selling like hotcakes. You know, the talk going around is that Como's going to sell a million of one of his sides."

The grin faded from Marlon's face, a strained look came into his eyes. "A million? How much does that mean for him?"

"Plenty. All a guy has to do is make a couple of those million-record sales and he don't have to worry for life." Shannon searched his pockets for a cigar, couldn't find one, went rummaging through the second drawer of the desk. "You know what the new gimmick is? They're pressing a solid-gold record for him. How about that?"

Marlon watched the older man take a cigar from the drawer, bite off the end. "So how much does the writer of the song get?"

"The usual. Three-three-fifty."

The thin man scowled at him. "I don't want tomorrow's lucky number. How much does the writer get?"

"Like I said. Three cents on every copy, three cents on every orchestration and fifty per cent of all other income."

"That's juke boxes, records, everything. Right?"

Shannon nodded. "The take from juke boxes for the writer ain't much. Even the artist don't get a royalty on juke box plays."

"Why not?"

"The mobs. They got the jukes tied up solid. They don't give out for anybody, ASCAP, BMI, anybody."

Marlon picked up a pencil from his desk, chewed on the end dreamily. "Even so, it means some real change if you got a hit record." He rolled his eyes over to Shannon. "How come we ain't got a hit record?"

"Maybe because we haven't written one."

"It's never too late." He cracked the pencil with his

teeth, spat splinters of wood at the wastebasket. "Maybe we ought to have a little talk with Arnie Cohen or some of the other boys."

"About what?"

"About us getting a hit record," Marlon growled. "Here we make these bums a potful of dough and what do we get for it?"

Shannon grinned. "None of them have been too ungrateful."

"Peanuts," the thin man snorted. "That's the trouble with this whole racket. It's been for peanuts up to now with schmoes like Marty Allen doing a big spin just for exercise."

"What's this I hear about Marty?"

Marlon shrugged elaborately. "He's getting some kind of a desk job."

"A real promotion, huh? One more like that and he'll be back on a corner selling apples."

"It's his own fault. He's so damned straight-laced that program of his has been putting them to sleep instead of waking them up. I'll fix that."

Shannon pulled the cigar from between his teeth. "You know, I never figured you for a guy who'd get up at six to do a show."

"I'm not. You think I'm crazy? Look, there's no reason for both the engineer and me to get up, so I had me an idea. I'm going to record the early show and they can use an announcer to give the time every fifteen minutes."

"Dickenson went for that?"

Marlon grinned. "Why not? I'm making money for him, ain't I? Marty Allen isn't making money, is he? Okay, so who's right and who's wrong?"

Shannon chewed on his cigar. "I see what you mean."

"Now to get back to Arnie Cohen—"

Shannon shook his head. "I don't know about that, kid."

"I didn't ask your opinion," Marlon told him coldly. "I want to have a talk with Arnie. All you've got to do is set it up."

"Okay."

"You know a Brill Building character named Joe Devine?"

"Yeah. A Poverty Row publisher. Had one big one about fifteen years ago and has been trying to live off it ever since."

"I want to see him, too. At my place."

"When?"

Marlon scowled at him. "That's up to you. Give me about forty minutes with Arnie before you send Devine in."

"You want them there together?"

"Yeah. But I want to soften Arnie up before Devine gets there."

There was a soft rap on the door. Marlon nodded for Shannon to open it. Ann Allen, Marty's redheaded wife stood in the doorway.

She smiled at Eddie. "Am I intruding?"

Eddie let his eyes roam over her full figure, grinned. "You're a lot prettier than Shannon. Him I can talk to anytime." He cocked his head at Mike. "You know what I want done, Mike. Have them at the apartment." He stared at the redhead speculatively. "If I get a change in plans, I'll let you know." He waited until the door had closed behind Shannon. "Now what can I do for you, honey?"

The redhead shook her head. "I just dropped by to congratulate you on your new morning program." She walked over to the desk. "I hear it's already oversold."

Marlon shrugged. "It figured. They're falling all over

themselves to get on it." He studied her curiously. "I figured you'd be a little peeved. Or maybe I had you wrong."

"Maybe."

He smirked, got up and walked over to her. "Don't tell me he's as big a stuffed shirt in bed as he is in front of a mike?" He slid his arm around her waist, pulled her against him. He was encouraged by her lack of resistance, got a little bolder. "There's nothing I can't do better than Allen, baby."

Her knee came up sharply; he released his hold on her with a grunt of pain. As he doubled up, his face came into range of a stinging open-hand slash that slammed him against the desk.

"You little rat," she snarled at him. "I wouldn't let Marty do this because I didn't want him to dirty his hands." The thin man was gasping air into his lungs, trying to get his breath. He shook his head weakly as she moved in, slashed the back of her hand across his face, snapping it back as though it were hinged.

"You're not even fit to breathe the same air Marty Allen does. And if you're figuring to get even with him for this, don't forget that I've got witnesses I came in here. And a girl has the right to defend herself against unwelcome passes." She grinned at him, picked up her bag, walked to the door and stood with her hand on the knob. "If I hear that you're giving Marty a bad time in any way, so help me I'll swear out a warrant for attempted rape and drag your filthy little name through every ounce of mud I can scare up."

Eddie Marlon let himself into his new, elaborate apartment, headed for the bathroom. He leaned over the basin, splashed cold water onto his face. One cheek had begun to discolor slightly and there was a long scratch from the stone in her ring. He swore long and volubly, planned all manner of revenge in his mind, but was aware as he did that he could not risk the redhead making good her threat.

The new apartment was a far cry from the shabby efficiency he had first occupied after going to work for Republic. It was a huge, modern, bachelor apartment that consisted of one mammoth room that was divided by a breakfast bar at one end, behind which nestled an efficient miniature kitchen. A large picture window overlooking the East River took up most of one wall, the rest of the room was a combination bedroom-living-room.

In the daytime two oversized couches lined the walls. There was a big fieldstone fireplace with a comfortable fire hissing and puffing on the hearth. At night the couches were drawn together, became a king-sized double bed. Lately it had been fully occupied.

When Arnie Cohen knocked at the door the next day, Eddie Marlon was sprawled on one of the couches, his mind rehearsing the conversation he intended to have with the A and R man. He got up from the couch, gave the fire a poke, ambled over to open the door.

Cohen nodded, walked in and tossed his hat at a table. He swabbed at his pink bald spot with a handkerchief. "A fire going yet. And on a day like this."

"I like fires," Eddie told him. He walked back to the couch, dropped onto it. "Glad you could come up."

"I was in the neighborhood," Cohen told him cautiously. "Shannon says you got something to talk over, I figure to drop by." He wheezed as he headed for the chair farthest from the fire. "Always glad to do business with you, Eddie."

"Thanks." Marlon reached over, picked a cigarette from a humidor, tapped it on the end table. "Especially if you make some money out of it?"

The fat man shrugged expressively. "I got to do business, why shouldn't I make a profit?"

"Have a drink?"

Cohen shook his head. There was a wary look in the eyes half veiled by the heavy-veined, discolored lids. He waited for the thin man to get to the point.

"I hear the record business is booming." Marlon lighted his cigarette, took a deep drag. "Some sides selling as much as a million."

"It should only happen to me."

"Tell me, Arnie, how does it work? I mean where do you fit in the over-all picture?"

"It's my job to pick what's commercial. I make a wrong pick, it's my neck."

"How can you tell a song's going to go or not?"

"Look, let's stop playing games, Eddie. Who should know better than you how a song clicks? Eddie Marlon gets behind it, that's better than it should rhyme June with moon."

"I hear some A and R men get a piece of a song every now and then."

The heavy lids almost covered the little black eyes. "It could be. Every day I hear peculiar rumors."

"I hear an A and R man can make or break a song by putting the wrong artist on it," Eddie continued. "Just to make sure they don't make that mistake, some publishers or writers give them a piece."

Bubbles formed and broke in the center of the fat man's lips as he puffed them in and out. "It figures a Frankie Laine can't sing soprano just like it figures Rosa Ponselle can't sing bass. So maybe sometimes a publisher does give somebody a present not to make mistakes. So you have a complaint?"

"Look, Arnie, you're not the only A and R man in the

business. I got a proposition. You're not going to level with me, I'll get next to somebody who will."

"What do you want to know?"

"I want a piece of a couple of songs. I want a writer credit on them."

The fat man rolled his eyes up, settled back, touched the tips of his fingers across his belly. "I saw that song you wrote when you were a kid. It was nowhere. You got another?"

Marlon shook his head. "You got the songs. You got the songs. You got hundreds of them. You pick the right ones for me to put my name on."

The fat man's jaw sagged. "You're not getting to me."

"You're not very bright today, Arnie," the thin man told him pleasantly. "It's not complicated. A writer or a publisher wants a record cut, right? He comes to you. You got the say on the artists in your house, whether they cut the song or not. Right?"

Cohen swabbed at his damp face, nodded.

"Okay, so instead of taking a petty larceny cut on the record, you'll fix it so you make some decent dough."

"How?"

"Suppose you tell the guy the record might go but the lyrics need fixing or the music needs a little doctoring. You got the guy for it, a guy who can not only fix the tune up but see that it gets a play."

Cohen ran the damp handkerchief around the inside of his collar. "You think they'll go for it?"

"Why not? This way they get a cutting by a big house, a name artist, and a guaranteed plugging. What's better, a hundred per cent of nothing or fifty per cent of a hit?"

"Not bad," the A and R man conceded.

"Then there's another angle that occurred to me.

There must be plenty of stuff comes your way without a big publisher to handle it or with some shoestring guy just giving it a fast ride on a demo."

"I'm up to my tail in that kind of stuff all the time."

"Any of it good?"

Arnie shrugged. "You want to work on it, give it a big background, stick a name artist out front on it, and then put up the dough for the promotion, some of it might go."

"Suppose we publish it?"

"We?"

"You and me. With a beard."

Cohen licked at his lips, tried to punch a hole in the idea, nodded cautiously. "We might make a buck."

"So okay. You know a shoestringer named Devine?"

"Devine Music? Strictly from hunger."

"So what's the difference between a publisher strictly from hunger and a publisher that's on top?"

"A couple of hits."

Marlon nodded. "Okay. I've got Joe Devine coming by here," he checked his watch, "in about half an hour. I haven't talked to him about this, but there's no doubt he'll jump at the chance."

"It might be risky."

"Where's the risk? You like a tune, you recommend a publisher you're used to working with. The publisher guarantees the song a top side, so who's going to argue?"

"Can we trust Devine? Some of the Poverty Row publishers—"

"We won't have to. We'll buy into his firm, take over control. He gets out of line, he's out." He waved aside an interruption. "And don't think Devine wouldn't prefer to have a piece of a going concern to that dust collector he's got now."

He was right, and it was less than a year before Devine Publishing, in conjunction with Rhythm Records presented crooner Morty Davis with a gold record for the job he did oil "Sugarbeat Time," Devine's first million seller. So, almost five years after the day he first walked into Joe Devine's office with his song under his arm, Eddie Marlon was big in the music business.

16

The feud between Eddie Marlon and Tony DeSales which had started at the Music Marathon grew in the months that followed, into a Radio Row legend. The rendition of DeSales's records on the shows controlled by Marlon was a standing gag in Lindy's, along Jacobs Beach, in the Brill Building, as well as among the teenagers who had become Marlon addicts.

DeSales attempted to hit back via a full-page ad in *Variety* in which he stated:

Open Letter to Eddie Marlon
It will be a long time before I have to win a pat on the back by giving my talents gratis to you or anybody else who uses them for his own good. Every other artist should join me in protesting the abuse of our talents under threat of blacklist or distortion.
(Signed) Tony DeSales

But it fell flat on its face when Eddie Marlon's answer appeared in full-page space in the next issue, asking simply:

Open Letter to Tony DeSales
What talent?
        (Signed) Eddie Marlon

It came to a head shortly after the second annual Marlon Music Marathon. That year artists actually fought to appear at the Garden, bands even offered to pay the costs of transporting instruments and effects from regular engagements so that they might contribute their time and talents.

Eddie Marlon and Mike Shannon had dropped by the Deadline Café on Madison Avenue after wrapping up the afternoon show. With the addition of the five-to-six segment, Eddie Marlon shows now constituted almost all of Republic's daytime programming. Yet the waiting line for sponsors continued to grow daily.

Marlon and Shannon were discussing a new phase of the Marlon Enterprises, a series of personal appearances at high school and college proms with top names of radio and records dropping by to make an appearance and staying long enough to do a number or two. Although there was no active resistance to this latest encroachment on their time, it was common gossip that many artists were complaining about the extra duties required to keep Eddie Marlon's good will.

By seven-thirty, Shannon's interest in the subject had waned and he was evidently working up interest in a redhead at the far end of the bar who gave signs of tiring of her date.

"Might get some action out of that, Eddie. Probably has a friend?"

Marlon studied the girl, considered it, shook his head. "You tackle it alone tonight, Mike. I'm bushed. I think I'll go back to the apartment and get some sack time." He dropped some bills and silver on the bar.

"One for the road, Mr. Marlon? On the house." The thin man considered it, decided no amount of liquor could lift him out of the mood he was in, shook his head.

The cool breeze felt good after the closeness of the bar. He looked up at the sky, decided it was a good night for walking. He was halfway up the block when the man came up behind him and tapped him on the shoulder.

"What's on your mind, friend?" Marlon asked.

The other man was dapper, almost pretty in an effeminate way. He was hatless and his hair, beginning to show signs of thinning at the temples, was light and wavy. "There's someone wants to see you," he said.

The disc jockey shook his head. "Some other time. I'm not feeling very sociable tonight." He started to turn away, was caught by the arm and spun back around.

"I think you ought to." The light-haired man's voice was low, intimate, almost as though he were whispering. "The next time he might send an invitation you wouldn't be in a condition to refuse."

Marlon felt a sinking in the pit of his stomach. He looked past the other man to the entrance to the Deadline Café, but Shannon's reassuring bulk was nowhere in sight.

"You make it hard to refuse." He worked at a grin with indifferent success.

The light-haired man raised a hand and signaled. A black sedan pulled away from the curb down the block and rolled toward them. It came to a stop at the curb and the back door swung open.

"We have a little way to go," the light-haired man explained. "Of course we'll also provide the transportation home."

Marlon shrugged, stepped in, and leaned back against the cushions. The other man followed, closing the door after him. He settled back in his corner, seemed to lose interest in his passenger.

The driver threaded the car through the early evening traffic, headed west to the elevated highway. Once there, he started downtown toward the Holland Tunnel.

"Jersey, eh?" Marlon dug his hand into his pocket, came up with a pack of cigarettes. "Still not going to tell me what this is all about?"

The other shook his head. He leaned over, held a lighter for Marlon's cigarette. "All I know is you're invited to a party."

"I'm not dressed for a party," the thin man grunted.

"This is a come-as-you-are party." The dapper man lapsed into silence again, watched the darkened piers glide by.

Marlon leaned back against the cushions, smoked moodily. The big car emerged on the Jersey side of the tunnel, headed for the Pulaski Skyway. The driver handled it with the ease of long experience, weaving it in and out of the slow-moving traffic, making time. Once past the Newark Airport, he took Route 22 toward Union.

The character of the neighborhood changed from densely populated to suburban, with bigger and bigger stretches of unpopulated areas showing up. About forty minutes from the Holland Tunnel, the driver swung off Route 22 onto a macadam road that meandered back for about a mile.

The Dude Ranch was a large, sprawling white-frame building. From the outside it gave no indication of its character, looked like any other large country estate that had been kept up. Shrubs and lawns were in good condition and it was only by the discreet brass nameplate on one of the gate pillars that it could be identified as the Dude Ranch.

The driver swung the big car between the two stone

pillars onto a crushed bluestone driveway that led to the house itself. He pulled up to a canopied entrance.

The light-haired man got out first, waited for Eddie Marlon, then followed him up the broad stone stair-case. A grilled metal door led into what had once been the house's reception hall.

Small groups of people in formal dress were already clustered in the hall, despite the early hour. A low murmur of polite conversation welled toward the two men as they entered the hall. Overhead a pall of smoke stirred restlessly in the draft from the open door.

"Upstairs," the other man told Marlon.

The door at the head of the stairs had the word *Private* stenciled on it in gold leaf. The light-haired man pushed the door open.

A man sat on the corner of a desk that looked as if it had cost important money. He didn't look up from the engrossing job of paring his fingernails. "Took you long enough, Al," he complained mildly.

"He didn't go right home, stopped in a bar. I had to wait."

The man on the desk looked up, nodded. "Okay. Go on down to the bar and buy yourself a drink. I'll call you when I need you."

Al nodded, closed the door behind him.

"I've been wanting to meet you, Marlon." The man on the desk snapped the knife closed, dropped it into his pocket. "My name's Johnny Endres. Maybe you heard of me?"

"I've heard about you." Marlon's eyes searched the face of the other man, found a similarity to the pic-tures of the notorious Jersey racketeer. The years had made a lot of changes in that face. The lean wolfish-ness of it was blurred by a soft overlay of fat. Flat, lusterless eyes peered from beneath heavily veined, thickened eyelids, but the soft, discolored pouches beneath them took away from the menace.

"What have you heard about me?"

Marlon shrugged. "You used to be a pretty big wheel in the rackets in the old days. Ran most of the Jersey mob. But now you're retired."

Endres laughed, exposed discolored teeth. "I still like to keep my hand in a couple of enterprises." He took a pack of gum from his pocket, carefully unwrapped a stick. "I suppose you're wondering what I had you brought out here for?"

Marlon nodded. He looked around the place. "I didn't know you owned this place."

"I don't. Crossan owns it. He lets me use it when I got personal business. Like tonight." He rolled the gum into a ball, stuck it between his teeth. "I want you to stop rapping Tony DeSales."

"What's in it for me if I do?"

"Maybe an accident if you don't. A real bad one."

Marlon felt the sinking sensation in his stomach at the matter-of-factness of the other man's voice. Endres sat chewing on the wad of gum with no change of expression.

"I got a lot of money tied up in that songbird, fellow. I don't like the way you been taking him on."

"Look, Mr. Endres, you got a right to make money, I got a right. This guy's been bucking me, so I hit back the only way I know how. He hits me in the take, I do my damnedest to hit him in the take."

"It's got to stop." Endres got down off the desk. "I ain't interested in the penny pitching you do." He grinned at Marlon. "I got some idea of how you been doing, shaking the singers, shaking a couple of record outfits. Okay. That's okay with me. Only don't get in my way."

"How am I hurting you?"

The cold black eyes regarded him for a minute. "It cost me a couple of bucks to build Tony into a top name. You know how? There are half a million juke boxes in this country. They do a billion a year. That's not peanuts, no?"

Marlon licked at his lips, shook his head.

"Okay. Me, Endres, I control the syndicate that runs the jukes. The same syndicate operates the big joints at Vegas. Places like this and the Sarasota in New York, they're all part of the chain. We make and we break our own stars. DeSales, he's one of our stars."

"I didn't know."

Endres bobbed his head. "Okay, so now you know. We got a lot tied up in a property like DeSales. It meant using muscle to spot his records number one and number two in the jukes. It meant pushing him down the public's throat at Vegas, here at the Sarasota. Okay, so now they got the idea they discovered this meathead—and I don't want somebody like you showing him up for the bum he is."

"Okay, Mr. Endres. I didn't know." Marlon wiped the dampness off his upper lip with the side of his hand. "How about DeSales, though?"

"He'll do what he's told." The heavy-faced man pushed at a hidden button on the desk. The door opened, Al stuck his head in. "Get Caruso."

They waited until Al returned, herding the singer in front of him. Tony DeSales wore exaggerated shoulders in his blue suit, a gray shirt with matching tie. His hair was heavily oiled, flat against the temples, a bunch of curls on the top. His complexion was sallow, his lips thick and sensuous. He had moist, cowlike eyes.

"This here's Eddie Marlon," Endres told the singer

without looking at him. "You and him's going to shake—"

"In a pig's eye, I am," DeSales growled. He started for Marlon, was deflected by an expertly thrown shoulder block by Al, staggered to the side. When he started for Marlon again, Endres moved with a speed surprising in a man his size.

He caught DeSales by the lapels, threw him back into a chair. Then he lashed out with his open palm, knocked the singer's head to one side, then backhanded it into position. "You gettin' deaf? I said shake on it."

"Okay, Mr. Endres, I'll shake on it." The singer cowered back in the chair.

"You'll do more than that, glamour boy," the gangster growled. "I got no interest in you except that you're an investment. Don't let all them screaming kids fool you into thinking you're a big star, sucker. You're just what I made you and the only thing that keeps me from breaking you is that I got too much time and money tied up in you."

DeSales's head rolled from side to side, finally fell to his chest.

"But don't let that fool you, sucker. Maybe I can make as much money from you dead as alive. You got plenty of records, records that'll sell after you're gone. Especially if something romantic happens to you. Something like disappearing, or shooting yourself over a lost love. It's happened, you know." He sank his fingers into DeSales's hair, pulled his head back. "Okay, so you shake hands with this guy and get whatever's with the two of you cleaned up."

That night, on the ride home from the Dude Ranch, Eddie Marlon mapped out in his own mind the explanation for calling off the feud. But even the best efforts of the publicity men from Consolidated Artists Service, who handled Tony DeSales, and the press department of Republic never were able to convince all of Radio Row that the feud had been no more than a publicity stunt along the lines of the Jack Benny-Fred Allen attention-getter.

But there was no denying the fact that the bitterness that once existed between the two was replaced by almost as fierce a camaraderie whenever they met in public.

17

The "understanding" with Tony DeSales and his backers paid off in more ways than one. After the hatchet had been publicly buried at one of Eddie Marlon's School Concerts, the new rapport was cemented further by the appearance of Tony DeSales at the senior prom at Boys High in Brooklyn. In return, DeSales's records started getting more and more play on the Eddie Marlon shows. To show his gratitude, Johnny Endres had pleased Eddie and his partners at Devine Music by slotting its current hit, "Moonlight Melody," in the number-one position of half the juke boxes around the country.

The only fly in Marlon's ointment was the number of "imitators" that had begun to crop up on every radio station across the country. When he had started the Eddie Marlon Show six years ago, there had been almost no competition. As the record industry got into full swing, more and more stations assigned time to disc jockeys and got on what Marlon firmly believed was his personal bandwagon. Although he was still admittedly the king of the disc jockeys, some of his absolute authority was being threatened by the very number of the imitators.

"It's not like the old days, kid," Mike Shannon complained, "Now when I tell them they either come through or we stiff them on the play, they laugh me off. If we don't play their sides, there's lots of others will. This market is getting lousy with disc jockeys, kid."

Even appearances by artists at the School Concerts and at the school proms (once command performances) started to drop off. Marlon found it harder and harder to put the muscle on them to appear. They complained that if they showed for an Eddie Marlon prom, they'd be bombarded with requests from other jocks to show for no.

"So, okay," Dinah Reed snapped at Mike Shannon one night at the Backstage Club. "So Eddie Marlon's got the knife out for me. So I'm dead in this town as far as his play goes. You think this is the only town in the country? Besides, let Marlon stiff me. There are plenty of others even in this town who won't. I'm through putting out for him."

"Worst part of it is, she's right," Shannon told Marlon gloomily. "We don't have the old whip anymore, kid. We want to stay on top, we got to come up with a new gimmick. One that'll really muscle them back into line."

"How about next Saturday's School Concert?"

Shannon shook his head. "Just a couple of schnooks. No names at all."

"How come that creep on WTLB got first crack at the new Rhythm side featuring the Coronets? That's a real comer."

Shannon managed to look unhappy. "Arnie gave it to him. Said you got tough about it and he had no budget, so he gave it to somebody who'd play it for free. It turned out to be a sleeper." He shrugged. "We can't get them all."

"We get them all," Marlon told him flatly. "We get all the firsts in this town." He pointed a finger at the other man. "They play with these two-bit spinners and when they fall flat and come crawling back to me, it's going to cost them double. You tell them that for me."

"I already told them. Nobody's falling flat, kid. You got to face it. These other guys are here to stay."

Marlon got up from his chair, paced the small office. "I'm not facing anything. This whole racket is my idea. I dreamed it up. And nobody's muscling in." He stopped in front of Shannon. "Or maybe you think I'm slipping, too."

"You're still king-pin, kid"—Shannon found a cigar, anchored it in its usual place—"but you got to accept the fact that now these guys have got somebody to turn to if you stiff them." He chewed on the cigar glumly. "If they start playing with these other guys heavy enough, could be we'll have trouble."

"How?"

"Word gets around that all the new numbers are breaking someplace else and the kids start tuning him in, we've had it." He waved off the sour look on Eddie's face. "We got no mortgage on these guys, Eddie. All they know is they got songs and they want a show-case. We don't give it to them, they go someplace else. Maybe for less."

Marlon walked around his desk, dropped into the chair. "You said something about a new gimmick."

"I was just tonguing," Shannon admitted. "If we could only get them back into line—"

"If I do," Marlon told him grimly, "I'm not forgetting

what's been going on. I got a little list and anybody on it is dead."

"We can't make it stick, kid." Shannon shook his head. "Not unless you got the idea of burning down all the other stations. They found out there's plenty of loot in spinning platters. You think they're going to get off the gravy train because you're unhappy?"

"Maybe I can make them unhappy."

"How?"

"How the hell do I know?" Marlon picked up a letter opener, dug at his nails. "There must be an angle."

"In bed I been spinning like a top trying to figure one. I don't think there is any."

"If we could only handle them like Johnny Endres handles the jukes." He looked up. "He's really got it made."

"How's he operate?"

"Nobody runs a juke without he gives the okay. They play the records he says they can play and they pay him for the privilege."

"Don't he pay the locations for letting him put the boxes in?"

"You crazy? The locations only get a commission. He gets the first twenty on the play. Then the rest of it's split sixty per cent for Endres and forty per cent for the location."

"You kidding?"

"Of course I'm not kidding. You know how that works out? The average juke does about $50 a week in a small spot. So Johnny gets the first $20, that leaves $30. He gets sixty per cent or $18 and the tavern guy gets $12."

"What a setup!"

Marlon tossed the letter opener back on the desk. "That's because he's organized, and—" He broke off, stared at Shannon.

"Okay, so he's organized."

Marlon caught his lower lip between his teeth, chewed on it for a moment, then he snapped his fingers. "Why can't we organize?"

"You mean the A and R men? The publishers?"

Marlon shook his head. "No. I mean the disc jocks."

"You nuts?" Shannon growled. "How could you organize a bunch of dog-eat-dog operators? You think they'd stand still for you running the deal?"

Marlon ignored him, got up and walked to the window. He stood for a moment, smoothing his hair, then he swung around. "One top platter spinner in every town. How about that?"

The frown that creased Shannon's forehead faded, was replaced by a speculative stare. "Oh, handle it like that, eh?"

"Yeah. They play tricks on us here in New York and we make sure they're stiffed all over the country." He walked back to his desk, grinned at Shannon. "How do you like that? They don't need me because they can get plays in other cities, eh? Okay, so suppose I cut them off from every big-time play across the country? What then?"

"You've got them by the neck." Some of Marlon's enthusiasm was beginning to seep into Shannon's voice. "Sort of a union."

"That's right. No, make it a fraternity. The companies hurt one of us, they hurt us all. I even got a name for it."

"What's that?"

"The Knights of the Round Table."

Shannon slapped his thigh, his bad humor completely dissipated. "I buy it."

Marlon reached for the phone. "I'll try it out on Dick

Lobe in Chicago. If he buys it—"

"Wait a minute," Shannon advised. "You'd better think it over. You don't want him to have any questions you can't answer."

"Like for instance?"

Shannon shrugged. "What's in it for him?"

"The same thing that's in it for me. It means he stays number one in his market. The disc companies start playing footsie with some other spinner, we give them the works all over the country."

"Now you've got it. That's your answer." Shannon chewed on his cigar excitedly. "We'll have them all back on their knees."

Marlon's mind was racing ahead. "We guarantee the Knights all firsts from every company in their market, talent that won't play ball on benefits and appearances gets the works, we have a clearing house on what's top in every market in the country."

"And?"

"And all this costs the disc companies money."

"Now you're talking, kid."

"Think they'll go for it?"

Shannon grinned. "Like a duck for water. You think you're the only one's been worrying about all the cheap competish? Hell, some of those guys on the small stations are so anxious to get new releases they're spoiling the companies. They play for no. We can straighten them out overnight."

"How about the talent? Will this help you keep them in line?"

Shannon winked. "They're going to be falling all over each other to get back in line. The first one will be that Dinah Reed bitch. I'll—"

Marlon shook his head. "I don't want her."

Shannon's face fell. "You're going to let her get away

with what she tried to pull?”

“She’s not getting away with anything.” Marlon leaned back, his lips twisted in an ugly expression.

“She’s riding real high with that last release, kid. Real high.”

“That’s her last one.”

“How do you figure?”

“As soon as the Knights are organized and start throwing their weight around, we’re going to have an S-list, and she heads it.”

Shannon frowned, shook his head. “I don’t get it.”

“Nobody on that list gets a play. Any A and R man who pushes a good number to anybody on that list stands to have all the rest of his releases stiffed.” He snorted impatiently at the frown on Shannon’s face. “Look, the A and R man picks the tune, decides who does it. Right?”

Shannon nodded.

“Okay, so Dinah Reed can only do blues numbers. She empties the place faster than a plague when she does ballads. Am I right?”

“Yeah.”

“Okay, so Arnie Cohen skeds nothing but ballads for her. Or else.”

Shannon sank back in his chair, rolled the dead cigar between his thumb and forefinger. “You think you can make it stick?”

“What’s Dinah Reed to Arnie? Just one singer. You think he’ll go up against us if we’re going to ruin every singer on his list by no plays? He’ll dump her so fast it’ll make even you dizzy.”

18

The idea for the Knights of the Round Table found an enthusiastic reception with key disc jockeys all over the country. In a matter of weeks, the organization was ready to function and Eddie Marlon had been delegated to acquaint the trade with its workings.

Monday was publishers' day at Rhythm Records. This was the day Arnie Cohen sat with an impassive face, listened to publisher after publisher play a few bars either on the piano or via demonstration record. Every Monday he heard a hundred songs, sometimes he okayed three, his average was two. Some of the publishers he knew, a fact that was demonstrated by a brief nod of the jowly head. Others he met with a cold stare of the beady black eyes. With none did he waste conversation.

Eddie Marlon walked into the reception room at Rhythm, told the girl behind the low railing that he wanted to see Cohen.

"Mr. Cohen sees nobody today. Today he listens to new material. I'm sure he—"

"Tell him Eddie Marlon wants to see him."

The girl looked dubious, permitted herself to be bull-dozed into checking via the switchboard. She mumbled a few words into the mouthpiece, then turned to Marlon. "He'll see you, Mr. Marlon. Do you know the way to the audition room?"

Marlon shook his head. The girl swiveled in her chair, pointed to the left-hand door behind her. "Down that hallway. There's a flight of stairs down to it. Brings you right into the audition room." She swung around. "Otherwise you'd have to fight your way through the crowd waiting in the downstairs reception room."

Marlon pushed through the gate set in the railing, entered the corridor. He had to pass a group of stenographers' desks to get to the stairway. A steep flight of winding steps led down to the big, barely furnished room where Arnie sat, dumped into an oversized armchair.

At the piano, a thin, eager little man with a bald head was pounding on the keys, singing nasally. When he finished, he turned around, studied the fat man anxiously. He said querulously, "It'd be a killer for Dinah Reed, Arnie. Right in her groove."

"Ain't doing anything with Dinah for a while." The fat man shook his head, disturbing the rolls of fat under his chin. "We don't want to cut the play on her new side." He sucked his pouty lips in and out for a moment. "Let me think about it, Morrie."

The little man bobbed his head, rolled up his music. "Don't take too long, Arnie," he pleaded. "I got a couple of other bites on it, but you know me, kid. I like doing business with you."

Arnie nodded. "I know you."

He waited until the little man had run from the room, turned to Marlon. "Hi, Eddie. You got me on a bad day. Got a lot of auditions set up."

"Call them off, Arnie." Marlon sat on the piano stool, stared at the fat man. "I want to talk to you."

A flicker of annoyance shadowed the fat man's face. "This is no place to talk, Eddie. Besides, Monday is audition day and I got a full—"

"Call it off." There was a hard note in the disc jockey's voice that made Cohen hesitate.

"Louise!" the fat man boomed. He didn't turn his head when the door to the reception room opened and a mousy-looking girl stuck her head in. "Tell them I can't listen to any more today. Tell them to come back next Monday."

As the girl turned and conveyed the messages, they could hear the roars of disappointment from the anteroom, then silence as the soundproofed door closed.

"Okay, Eddie. What's the fever?"

"I don't like the way you've been pushing me around lately, Arnie," Marlon began. "I especially don't like the attitude that bitch Reed has been taking."

The fat man blew bubbles in the middle of his lips. He shrugged. "She's hot. She don't feel she's got to kiss anybody's feet anymore."

"I figure to cool her off." Eddie swung on the stool, jabbed at a few notes with his index finger. "There are going to be a lot of changes made, Arnie." He looked up from the piano at the fat man. "A lot of changes."

The fat man laced his fingers across his stomach. "It's not like the old days, Eddie. Back five-six years ago you had the field to yourself, so you snap a whip, everybody jumps. Now it's different. The important thing is to get a play. Who by ain't important as long as the disc keeps getting a play." He shrugged again. "When you had the field to yourself was one thing. Now with every station in the country lousy with disc jocks, getting a play's a breeze."

Marlon fingered the keys for a moment, then brought his hands down hard on them. "Suppose I tell you that if I say so, any one of your releases is dead from one end of the country to the other?"

The fat man studied his face, shook his head slowly. "I'd say you couldn't make it stick. So okay. You stiff me here in New York. I can get the side skedded by half a dozen good boys. Not big like you, maybe, but coming up. Out of town—"

"Out of town you'll be dead. Just like here. Sure, you'll be able to pick up a few plays from the smaller guys. But how often? Often enough to do you any good if the key man in every market marks you lousy?"

Cohen looked uneasy. "Look, kid, don't make it personal with me. I got nothing against you. I always played ball. No?"

"You always played ball," Marlon told him pleasantly, "when you had to."

The fat man sighed. "Okay, so if I can get off the hook, do you blame me if—"

"You can't get off the hook. Look, Arnie, I'm going to lay it out for you. There's a new organization and I'm running it. We call it Knights of the Round Table."

"Jocks?"

Marlon nodded. "The top spinner in every market. We're working together. All the way."

Cohen licked his pouty lips. "Good, good. If I can—"

"You not only can. You either do or you're dead."

"Now wait a minute, Eddie. I got nothing against you guys getting together. I'll co-operate every way I can. But muscle I can't take. It's not like the old days. The company's cutting down, and—"

"You didn't let me finish," Marlon told him coldly. "We're making up a list. It don't pay to be on that list, Arnie, and like a good friend I'm giving you advance warning. Anybody on that list is on his way out. You know why?"

Perspiration glistened on the fat man's forehead. He shook his head.

"Because if you're on that list, nobody in the organization plays any disc that carries your label. We'll stiff everything you turn out, and we'll tell the artists why they're being stiffed."

Cohen licked at his lips. "What about the independent deejays? They won't go along with that. They'll still—"

"They'll still give you a spin. At first. Maybe you can make it with the Indies on your team. Me, in your shoes, I wouldn't want to take the chance." Marlon flashed a smile that didn't quite reach his eyes. "The boys figure we ought to have a horrible example to get off to a real start. I'm having trouble talking them out of using you."

"What could they do to me?"

"I just told you. Run you out of the business by putting the finger on any song or any artist you've got anything to do with. Once the word gets out that the only plays you can get are with a few local spinners—"

"What are you doing this to me for?" Arnie's voice reached a shrill pitch. "I always been all right with you guys. I been—"

Marlon shrugged. "It's got to be somebody. And lately I get the feeling you been giving me the business. This I don't like."

The fat man dug into his pocket for a balled handkerchief, swabbed at his face. "That's crazy. Who you been listening to? We're partners, ain't we?"

"Are we? I heard about that side Dinah Reed did, 'Come Hold Me Always.' It's headed for a pretty big sale." He reached into his pocket, brought out a battered pack of cigarettes. "How come Devine Music didn't get it, Arnie?"

The fat man shrugged. "Just one of those things, kid. We can't get everything."

"What do you mean 'we'? I hear you're cut into it."

"Cut in?" Cohen looked aggrieved. "What kind of cut? I helped fix up the lyric and so the kid who wrote it gave me a piece. A small piece. Honest."

"You took it to Mohawk Music. Did Bobby Sewell

over there give you a small piece, too?" He drew on the cigarette, blew the smoke at the ceiling. "You figured I was through, Arnie, and you figured wrong."

"That's crazy, kid. I just—"

"You just made a mistake. A big one." The thin man's gaze moved down from the ceiling to the damp face of the fat man. "And I'm going to prove it to you, buddy boy. I'm going to scuttle the Reed side just to give you an example of what can happen."

"You're going to scuttle 'Hold Me'?" Cohen shook his head. "You just said yourself it's headed for a big sale."

"It is. But not the Rhythm waxing."

Cohen looked stricken. "What are you saying? It's a Dinah Reed side and she's hotter than a fifty-cent pistol."

"She's dead." Marlon shook his head. "Any of them that don't play ball are dead. You want to know why?"

The fat man stared at him. "Why?"

"I just came from Mike Sabell at Tower Records. He's doing a cover of 'Hold Me' with Sally Lee. They're starting to press next week."

The fat man grimaced. "Sally Lee? She ain't in the same class with Reed. Sabell's wasting—"

"If 'Hold Me' hits a million, and I think it could, it will be the Lee side that does it." Marlon left the cigarette in the corner of his mouth, where it waggled when he talked. "The Knights have decided that we like the Lee version. We're going to give Sally's side the big spin—three or four times a day. All over the country."

Cohen slumped back in his chair, looked stricken. "It could hurt," he conceded. "But you can't stop the play on the indies, and—"

"Okay, that's your gamble. If you think a spotty play on a lot of small watters can stand up to a concentrated play on every high-rated disc show in the country, okay, you can try it. But if you do, you're out for good. We keep stiffing everything you touch and anybody you touch. Maybe you can make it without us, but we're sure going to give you a run for it."

The fat man licked at his lips, considered. "You could cost me my job."

Marlon nodded, grinned bleakly. "Yeah."

"How much time I got to think this over?"

"All the time you want, as long as I know you're in or out right now. Because if you're out, there are a couple of other sides you been pushing that we're probably going to want covers on."

The fat man sighed, shook his head. "I'm not going to fight you."

Marlon nodded, dropped his cigarette to the floor, crushed it out. "I didn't think you would." He stared at the fat man for a moment. "Here's what we expect: we want first crack at every new release in our market."

"But the other guys—"

"You want to play with them? Be my guest. I'm giving you a chance to get on the bandwagon, but if you want to play with the two-bit spinners on the small stations"—he shrugged—"it's your funeral."

Cohen swabbed at his face. "Okay. What else?"

"I'll provide you with a list of our members for your Christmas list. The boys have expensive tastes." He pursed his lips, considered. "I guess that's all except that we'll expect any of your artists in town to drop by for a personal appearance with the member in that town. Not only for his radio program, but any other show he's handling on the side."

Cohen nodded. "We'll go along." He wiped his palms with the balled handkerchief. "About Dinah Reed, Eddie. She ain't a bad kid. Maybe she could make it right. Maybe if she came over to your place tonight she could straighten things out—"

"Sorry, Arnie. Like I told you, we need a horrible example. Some of the companies might balk about getting into line. We're going to do a real job on Reed just to show them how bad it can get. When they see how bad it can get, they'll get the flash."

Dinah Reed hadn't always been a featured vocalist for Rhythm Records. She had come up the hard way; she had years of barnstorming the country with one small band after another behind her. She had done her share of one-night stands, singing her heart out in poorly ventilated clubs, dance halls with poor acoustics, dingy theatres and drafty gymnasiums.

The big one had come unexpectedly when the band she was singing with that season drew a recording date for Taos Recording. It was strictly instrumental, but on the jump side they featured a vocal by Dinah Reed that caught the attention of the big brass at Rhythm Records. Almost before she knew what was happening, she was signed by Rhythm and, with its promotional muscles behind her, she was fast becoming the country's favorite female recording star.

She had married once, a fact that she wanted desperately to forget. He had been a sideman in Ernie Bellows's band, a hotheaded, high-spirited kid who got on a dope kick that ruined his life and almost ruined hers.

Every so often, when it rained, she was reminded of him. It had all started in a dingy little hotel in Peoria. She had just joined the band and nobody had given her much of a tumble. It was a rainy Thursday and she sat in the tiny hotel room assigned to her, watching a black rain pour down on the city. The night before it had been raining, too, and they had played to a pitifully small house. Ernie Bellows claimed he had heard the promoter discussing the possibility of canceling out if the rain continued through today.

She had been trying to reconcile the glamour she had imagined she would share as the member of a touring band with the dinginess of her surroundings when Jimmy had knocked on her door.

He was tall and pale, with an unruly shock of pitch-black hair. The dark circles under his eyes and the petulant droop of his full lips had given him an air of excitement.

"Thought you might be lonely," he said when he opened the door in response to her invitation to come in. "Got anything to read?"

She shook her head. "I've just been watching the rain run down the window. Bet it's the first time it's been washed this year."

"I was going across to the diner for some coffee. Bring you back some?"

"I'll go with you. I like to walk in the rain."

"Good." He waited while she slipped into a coat, tied a scarf over her head. "Think this will keep up all day?"

"It better not or I'll be back behind the ribbon counter if what Ernie heard was true." She joined him in the hall, headed for the stairs. "If we get less of a crowd than we had last night, we'll be playing to ourselves."

The rain was cold and refreshing after the closeness of the hotel room. He caught her by the hand and they ran across the rain-drenched street, stamped into the steamy warmth of the diner. They shared a booth and got to know each other that afternoon.

There wasn't much to know about Dinah, she protested. She had grown up in Scranton, learned that she had a voice when she sang in the choir. The choirmaster had urged her to apply herself to developing her voice, had even volunteered his services and partial financing of her lessons. After a particularly nasty interlude in the choir loft she had left Scranton and headed for New York. Ernie Bellows had heard her on an amateur hour and had offered her a spot with his band, and here she was.

Jimmy's full name was James Tunnell. He had been with Ernie since the band was organized three years before. Now, he was getting itchy feet to make a change, to hit for the big time. He had an audition scheduled with Sammy Kaye when the band reached Chicago and he was anxious to make good. Sammy had heard him once and had encouraged him to come see him the next time he got to town. That was where he was heading, the big time.

But it took longer for Ernie Bellows and his band to get to Chicago than they had expected and by the time they got there, Sammy Kaye's orchestra had left on a tour that was to last several months.

By now, Jimmy and Dinah had become a Thing in the band, and the other members kept hands off. They were planning to marry as soon as he made the big time with Sammy Kaye, and if there was no room for her as a vocalist with Kaye, she would go on with Bellows's band until it returned to Chicago. Missing the audition had been a bitter pill for Jimmy to swallow, and he took to brooding about the lousy breaks fate always seemed to deal out to him.

When Ernie Bellows and his band started out again on tour, Jimmy decided to make a change. The Perry Howe band wasn't much bigger than Ernie's, but it was a step in the right direction, he told Dinah. They could get married now and he'd go on the road with Perry Howe; she would stay with Ernie until they had put aside enough money for her to stop working for a while.

She heard from Jimmy regularly for the first three months, then the letters came less frequently, were shorter and usually self-pitying. Finally she went to Ernie, laid the whole story out, and asked his permission to leave the band long enough to catch up with Jimmy and find out what was wrong.

When she finally did reach him, in a Kansas town where the Howe band was playing a split week, she learned that he had got on a heroin kick, that now he was a confirmed addict. She gave up her spot with the Bellows band to stay with him in an attempt to get him off the kick.

It had failed, as everyone assured her it would. Instead of getting better, Jimmy had become progressively more undependable. He hocked everything he could lay his hands on to get the stuff; finally Perry Howe had to admit to Dinah that he'd carried her man as far as he could. He was letting him out and his advice to her was to bail out herself.

Jimmy promised time after time to go to Lexington and kick the habit, but always chickened out when the time came. When she finally got him institutionalized, she wired Ernie Bellows, told him the situation and asked his help.

Jimmy stayed in the hospital three weeks, then signed himself out and headed for Chicago. In a black mood of self-pity, he wrote a letter to Dinah threatening suicide. She took the first plane for Chicago.

For days she haunted all the spots he used to frequent when in Chicago. She drew blank after blank until one day she met a piano player who had been with the band when she first joined it. He had seen Jimmy only a day or so before at a community joy-pop.

He gave her the address, warned her not to try going there without company. But she headed directly for the address, which turned out to be in a row of dingy frame buildings. It was the only house in the row that gave signs of ever having been painted.

Dinah crossed to the small stoop that led to the vestibule, walked up. As she pushed open the door, she became aware of a dull, monotonous beat that made the old place vibrate.

"Looking for someone, lady?" A heavy-shouldered man with a fedora on the back of his head materialized out of the gloom of the inner hall.

"Yeah. Jimmy Tunnell."

The man lighted a match. By its weak glare she could see the bristle of his unshaven chin, small beady eyes. He gave off a sour, fetid smell. "Who are you?"

"I'm married to Jimmy. Is he here?"

The man studied her for a moment, shrugged, indicated the stairs. "Upstairs." He squinted at her. "He expecting you?"

She nodded. "He asked me to meet him here."

At the top of the stairs, a heavy black drape sealed off the room behind. In the corridor the dull pounding was dimly identifiable as a drum. She pushed back the curtain, found the knob and opened the door. As she stepped into the room the wild beat of the music struck her with almost physical force.

She stood in a huge, dimly lighted room. Heavy drapes covered the walls from floor to ceiling, and on the floor a thick pile rug completed the soundproofing. In one corner a group of musicians were frenziedly pounding out a wild jungle beat.

A tall brunette danced wildly in the middle of the floor, her hair flying, her body twisting and undulating in time to the music. As Dinah watched, the girl's motions became more and more abandoned, until with a wild scream, she collapsed in a heap on the floor, lay there. Nobody paid any attention to the girl.

Dinah looked around the room, failed to see Jimmy. He was not among the musicians beating out the throbbing rhythm. Suddenly the door to the lavatory opened and he stepped out. In his hand he held a gleaming hypodermic.

She headed across the floor, was almost to him when he seemed to see her for the first time. His eyes widened, a tic developed under his right eye.

"Jimmy!" she ran toward him.

He seemed in terror at the sight of her, backed away until the wall was at his back. Then, as she continued toward him, he screamed, dashed quickly for the door by which she had entered.

"Jimmy! Wait for me," she screamed.

He didn't seem to hear as he tugged open the door, sprinted out into the hallway. There was a shrill scream, a loud series of thuds, then silence. It seemed to electrify the small group in the room. The music, which had been reaching for new heights of frenzy, broke off with a suddenness that made the silence an almost tangible thing.

As Dinah ran across the room, they stared at her with vacant eyes. Jimmy lay at the foot of the stairs, a tangle of arms and legs. From the angle of his neck, the open eyes that stared up sightlessly at the ceiling, she knew he was dead.

For the first time in too long there was a look of peace on his face.

After Jimmy's death, Dinah sang with one small

band after another. One town was the same as the next, and if it hadn't been for the lucky waxing of the side that brought her to the attention of the brass at Rhythm Records, she probably would have been content to spend her life in one-night stands.

With each succeeding record, she became bigger and bigger, until "Come Hold Me Always" showed unmistakable signs of becoming a gold-platter seller.

In her experience, men like Eddie Marlon meant little or nothing. They were just small-timers, spinning records. They had no background of music, they had no touch of the greatness of men like Jimmy Tunnell. They were parasites living off the talent of others.

19

Despite the fact that Dinah Reed's waxing of "Hold Me" had a substantial start on the cover version Tower put out with Sally Lee, it was the Lee side that became the standard. By the time the song reached the Hit Parade months later, it was pretty generally conceded that the Sally Lee version, which had racked up innumerable plays on the major disc shows throughout the country, had played a major job in pushing it to the top.

As word got around of what was happening, Dinah Reed found it harder and harder to make contact with the very bookers who had, a few months before, been bidding for her time. Although she waited patiently, Rhythm failed to come up with a suitable number to follow "Hold Me."

She sat in Arnie Cohen's office, a horsy-faced woman, her ash-blond hair cut close to her head. "What's happening, Arnie? We had a real one going for me in 'Hold

Me.' You promised to get behind it and make it big. It hardly gets any play at all. What happened?"

Cohen sat behind his desk, fidgeted with a letter opener. "You got the finger on you, baby."

"Who?"

"The disc jocks."

"That's crazy. I never did anything to the boys. Most of them are friends of mine. All the boys at WNEW give me a break, and—"

"I don't mean those boys, baby. I mean the mob Eddie Marlon has lined up behind him."

"Marlon, Marlon. That's all I hear. So all right, so I did tell that stooge of his I wasn't working any of his personal-appearance shows. So what is he, God Almighty?"

The fat man studied her. He liked the way she filled the Nile green sweater, the way the tweed skirt clung sheathlike to her long legs. "He may not be God Almighty, baby, but he packs a lot of weight in this business. With the key boys in the other markets playing ball with him, he pretty near makes it or breaks it."

"But they're not the only ones in the business. How about all the others?"

Cohen shifted uneasily. "They're not organized, baby. Sure, they give you a spin now and then, but nothing like the way the Marlon mob got on Sally Lee's side and rode it. Pretty soon, even the guys not in the setup start getting requests for Sally Lee. You know how that goes."

"You mean it's going to be the same with my next record?"

The fat man dug into his drawer, brought out a fresh pack of gum. "You got them on your back, baby. I think we'll wait a little while before you cut another side.

Maybe it'll cool off."

"You crazy? You think I'm going to let you put me on the shelf just because you're afraid of Marlon?"

He unwrapped a stick of gum, rolled it into a ball, stuck it between his teeth. "You got a better idea?"

"Yeah. I want out on my deal. I'll go someplace else and—"

"Look, baby, you don't know the score. The word's out you head the list. The other outfits, they see what goes. They know Marlon and his boys cut you down on 'Hold Me' and they'll be laying for anything else you do. If we can take a hosing on a sure hit like 'Hold Me,' what do you think they can do to us on a just so-so song?"

"Well, what do you expect me to do?"

Cohen pursed his lips, let bubbles form and break in the middle of them. "You better get next to Marlon, baby. Get the heat turned off. As long as the finger's on you, kid, no company's going to take a chance."

"Look, I'm no kid, Arnie, but if you think I'm going to crawl in bed with that little crumb just to—"

Cohen shook his head. "It wouldn't do no good. You're not his type. He told me so." He chomped on the gum. "Your best bet is to work on Shannon."

"How?"

"How else?"

The blonde made an expression of distaste. "He's an old man, Arnie."

"Yeah. An old man, but with young ideas. And what's more important, he's an old man who can get next to Eddie Marlon."

"I won't do it."

The fat man shrugged. "Somebody's telling you to do something? You ask me a question, I give you the answer. Marlon's got it in for you and until he takes the heat off, none of his gang will spin your sides. So the smaller local boys give you a spin and Marlon's mob clobbers it with a cover from some other company. You get hurt and we take a hosing. That's sensible?"

"But you could fight them."

Cohen considered, shrugged. "Maybe. Maybe not. In the meantime, it's costing the company important money. About this the company is very narrow-minded. We cut any more sides with you, we got a fight on our hands that can hurt us. So for a while, we—"

"You're going to let him run me out of the business?" the blonde asked with disbelief.

"You mean we got a choice?" Cohen touched the tips of his fingers across his belly. "I just finished telling you, baby, anybody touches you got a fight on his hands. This we need?"

"It's crazy, Arnie," the blonde cried. "Nobody should have the power to ruin somebody else's career like that. And you won't even fight back."

"Who can fight City Hall?" Arnie shrugged. "You been around. You know how things happen. As long as he can make or break a song, we've got to let him run things. If it ain't him, it's somebody else."

The blonde stood up, smoothed her skirt over her thighs. "I'm going to try."

The fat man scowled. "You're going to try what?"

"Do what you said. Fight City Hall."

"Just an expression, baby, just an expression. Nobody fights City Hall and wins. You're in a spot where nobody can help. Nobody except maybe Shannon."

Marty Allen was perched on a stool at Murphy's when the blonde slid onto the seat beside him.

"Coffee, Murph," she told the counterman.

"Hi, Dinah," Allen grinned. "Long time no see."

She waited until the counterman had slid a cup of coffee in front of her and shuffled away. "Marty, you know what Marlon's doing to me?"

Marty shook his head. "I haven't been keeping up with the scarlet career of the Pied Piper these past few years, baby." He patted his stomach. "Weak stomach."

"He's had me blacklisted."

When Allen scowled his lack of comprehension, Dinah Reed told him the setup of the Knights of the Round Table. He looked serious, shook his head.

"That sounds like a tough combination to lick, baby." He raked his fingers through his hair. "So now he's spread out on a national scale? God help the music business."

"God help them is right. They sure show no signs of helping themselves."

"They don't have much choice, Dinah. After all, you know what kind of an investment they put in every song they get behind. Why should they tie that kind of money up when it's a cinch that a handful of men like Marlon can kill the number? What would you do?"

"Then you think I'm finished, too?"

Allen sipped at his coffee. He picked up his cigarettes from the counter, held one out to the girl. "What'd you do to him?"

Dinah held the cigarette for a light, filled her lungs with smoke. "I got sick and tired of jumping every time he snapped his fingers. Shannon dropped by one night and told me he expected me at a School Concert at Thomas Jefferson High way the hell over in Brooklyn, yet." She shrugged, let the smoke escape through half-parted lips. "I told him I wouldn't show."

Marty nodded. "That would do it. Eddie couldn't stand for a defection in the ranks. It might give others ideas."

"I didn't realize he was so powerful."

"What happened with Tony DeSales should have tipped you off, baby."

"They made up, didn't they?"

Allen nodded. He lighted his cigarette from the one the girl held. "On Eddie's terms. You notice that De-Sales shows up at the concerts and at proms now. Even with the powerful backing DeSales has in Johnny Endres, he had to come to Marlon. And Marlon probably expects you to, too."

"It's not that simple. I'm not his type." The girl smoked moodily for a moment. "Even if I were, I don't think I could knuckle under to him anymore."

"What do you plan to do?"

The blonde shook her head. "I don't know. Isn't there some place I could go, something I could do to break his hold?"

"Federal Trade Commission, maybe. Complain that he's practicing restraint of trade, maybe. Or maybe you could appeal to the finer instincts of John K. Dickenson, the great president of Republic Broadcasting. Or tell your troubles to Mike Otto down at *Radio Confidential*. Any one of them could do the job, but I don't think they will." He signaled for a fresh cup of coffee. "I think we'll just have to grin and bear it."

"He gave you a dirty deal, too, didn't he, Marty?"

Allen shrugged. "Maybe I did it to myself, baby. Maybe I should have spotted him for what he was and got rid of him." He tapped the ash from his cigarette. "I guess I have no reason to blame Eddie. I've got a desk and a secretary. I work decent hours and see my family more often."

"But you were happier running the Early Morning Show?"

"I guess so. But I was a lot younger then, and so was this business. I guess I wasn't geared high enough to really play in Marlon's league." His coffee came, he stirred it absently. "You see, I don't blame Eddie Marlon for what's going on. He's not the disease, he's only a symptom of it."

"How do you mean?"

He tried his coffee, burned his tongue, swore softly. "Why do you think Marlon's the way he is? Because the A and R men, the publishers, and yes, even the artists themselves have made him that way. They tried to buy short cuts to a successful waxing by buying him. They made him so important in determining the success or failure of a song that one day they woke up to the fact that they'd created a full-grown monster."

"That still doesn't help me."

Allen shook his head. "Nothing's going to help you, baby, or me or the music business or radio until someone comes along to break the hold of guys like Marlon." He took a deep swallow of the coffee. "And that ain't likely to be soon."

20

Dinah Reed made her way through the organized confusion of desks that is the city room of the *New York Standard*. Men and women were sitting in front of typewriters of all makes and all vintages punching stories out for the next edition. From off in a room to the right came the insistent beat of the teletypes with an occasional ping to underscore an important item.

She walked to the back where two men were chopping copy, two others were leaning back, staring around the room with bored eyes. A thin man with tired, baggy eyes, a green shade pulled low on his forehead sat at a desk apart, checking the opposition papers for follows, throwing the mutilated copies into a barrel-sized wastebasket at his elbow.

"I'm looking for the editor," Dinah addressed him.

He put aside the paper he was checking, pushed the green shade high on his forehead, studied her. "I'm the editor on the city side. What can I do for you?"

"I want you to break up a racket," she told him. "Everybody else is afraid to, but you could do it."

"A racket?" There was a gleam of interest in the tired eyes. "What kind of a racket?"

"A shakedown."

He looked around the room, his gaze lighted on Sam Raskin. He nodded for Sam to come up to the desk. "I've got a man you can tell the story to, Miss—?"

"Reed. Dinah Reed."

The man behind the desk frowned. "Name sounds familiar. Should it?"

The blonde managed to look pleased. "I'm a singer. Maybe you heard my latest release. It's a thing called 'Come Hold Me Always'."

The man behind the desk bobbed his head. "I've got a couple of teen-age kids. That's all they do, play the record player." He turned to Sam Raskin. "This is Dinah Reed, Sam. She thinks she's got something the paper can get its teeth into. Want to tackle it?"

Sam Raskin looked the blonde over, appeared to like what he saw. "Sure, Mr. Hughes. What's it about?"

"Pull the lady up a chair and she can tell us about it." He waited until Dinah Reed was seated across from him and Sam Raskin was perched on the corner of the desk, and then he dug a battered briar from the top drawer, nodded. "Let's have it."

"You may think I'm raising all this fuss because I'm being blacklisted and that I wouldn't open my mouth if it was happening to someone else," she started, "but that's not so. I don't think a thing like this should be permitted to happen to anybody."

Hughes dug the bowl of his pipe into a pouch, started packing it with his index finger. He waited without comment.

"Did you know that any singer or any band can be broken overnight if they don't pay tribute?" She looked from Hughes to Raskin and back. "Everybody knows there's a payola in radio and television, but nobody knows just how big it is. And I think they should."

"So do I." Raskin held up a pack of cigarettes to her, waited until she had selected one, provided a light. "Want to tell us the whole story?"

Dinah took a deep drag, exhaled. "I don't know really where to begin. It's like a vicious circle. It doesn't start any place, it doesn't end any place—it just keeps going around."

"Well, why don't we start with the assumption that neither Mr. Hughes nor I know anything about the music business," Raskin suggested. "Suppose you trace us how a song becomes a hit or a flop."

The blonde picked a fleck of tobacco from the tip of her tongue. "It's not as accidental as it may sound. I mean you don't just cut a side and pray that the public will like it. The public don't pick the hits. They're picked for them and fed to them."

"How?"

"Repetition, promotion." She stared at the newsman. "You ever hear kids running around singing 'Pepsi-Cola Hits the Spot'? You think it's because it's great music? It's because they hear it so often it sticks to them. That's the same way a hit song makes it."

Raskin flicked a glance at Hughes and back to the girl. "I see. And who decides whether a song is going to get this concentrated play?"

"Well, it really starts with the A and R man at the recording house."

Raskin reached over, picked up a sheaf of copy paper and a pencil. "The A and R man, eh? What's he do?"

"He's the artists and repertoire manager of the company. He selects the songs the company will cut and then he decides what artists should do what songs. He keeps his eyes and ears open for the best songs the company's contract singers can get. He can make you or break you."

"By assigning you the wrong type songs?"

"Or not assigning any. But mostly by handing you a lemon. You know it's just as easy to ruin an artist by a flock of bad ones as it is to make a star with one good one."

Raskin scribbled some notes on the paper. "He sounds like a very important man."

"He is. If you're a publisher or an artist you make sure to remember his birthday, his kid's birthday, his wife's birthday and a lot of birthdays he doesn't even have."

Hughes tamped tobacco into the bowl of his pipe with his thumb, scratched a wooden match on the underside of the desk. "I can see how an artist would have to cater to the A and R man to get the best songs, but why must a publisher?" He held the match to the pipe.

"Today a publisher has to have a record outlet for his songs. The days when he made his through sheet music is gone. Some publishers are so anxious to get their songs waxed they'll cut an A and R man in on a tune. That way they're sure of a waxing and a hard push."

"Sounds like the A and R men have it all their own way."

"It's not all take for them. They have to do their share of kicking back, too."

"To band leaders and singers to plug the songs."

"Some. But the artists aren't as important as they used to be. Today the big push on a side comes from the disc jockeys. They're the boys who can make a side or break it." The blonde took a deep drag on her cigarette, let the smoke dribble from half-parted lips. "They're the boys who, by playing a tune over and over, can get the public going around humming it like it was a Pepsi-Cola jingle. Or they can stiff it and it lies dead."

"So they in turn put the heat on the A and R men?"

"And on the artists, too."

"Why?"

"There's usually more than one waxing of a good number. If they like you, they play your side. If they don't like you, they play somebody else's."

The reporter and city editor exchanged glances. "You have to pay off. Is that it?"

The blonde pursed her lips, shrugged. "Not exactly. I mean, the company that did the side usually picks up the tab for the number of plays. But there are other things—presents or personal appearances at the dee-jay's pet grafts."

Raskin scribbled a few lines. "Such as?"

"The usual stuff. They grab off all the glory by promising to produce us at benefits and special performances where they are getting paid to emcee. Like high school proms, for instance. Things like that. You either show, or they stiff your sides."

Raskin nodded for the girl to continue.

"Some even go on the make for the girl singers. A kid on the way up, she gets a proposition from one of these guys, it looks like a short cut, so she plays. That makes it tough on the rest of us."

"You didn't go along?"

"Look, you're in the racket, you do everything you have to do to make it. Once you're on top, you figure you don't have to pay the same tab you paid on the way up. I figured I had it made with 'Hold Me.' "

Raskin looked up, frowned.

"Her last big recording," Hughes explained.

"That was about six months ago. It was going great. Then Mike Shannon, one of Eddie Marlon's leg men—"

"Marlon? I know a little about him. He show in this?"

"Show in it? This is his life story." Dinah took a deep drag on her cigarette, marshaled her thoughts. "Shannon told me Marlon expected me to show at a prom he had booked that Saturday night. All the way over in Brooklyn, yet. And for no."

"For no?"

"No dough. I told Shannon I didn't have to put out like that anymore and he got sore. What's the matter, he says, you think you're too big? Just remember who made you big—Marlon—and he can cut you down to size any time he wants to. That's what he said to me."

"You stuck to it?"

"I told him to get lost. I figured a couple of years ago he could maybe make it stick, but not now. I'm riding too high with 'Hold Me' for him to hurt me. So he won't play me? Okay, there's plenty of other guys on local stations who will. Right in this town, too. Not as big as Marlon," she conceded, "but a play's a play."

Hughes rattled the juice in the stem of his pipe. "Then why should a man like Marlon pull so much weight?"

"Because he was away ahead of all of us." She dropped her cigarette on the floor, crushed it out. "He set up a co-op deal with key deejays all over the country. Almost like a union. One guy puts you on his list, all of them have you on the list. And you get no play."

"Certainly every disc jockey in the country isn't in it?"

"No. Just a key man in every market."

"But you can still get played by the independents."

"It helps. But it's not enough."

Raskin scratched at his head. "I don't understand why not. You just said a play's a play."

"It is. But the way they handle it, they clobber you. Take 'Hold Me' for instance. They decide to kill my side of it, so they get another singer to do the same song. On 'Hold Me' it was Sally Lee for Tower." She grinned bleakly. "Even with the head start I had with my side, she's outselling me ten to one."

"But how?"

"Marlon and his group have been skedding her side three and four times a day. Really getting behind it. The independents, maybe they give me a play every other day. They have no ax to grind so they treat my side like any other. Pretty soon, like the kids singing 'Pepsi-Cola Hits the Spot,' Sally Lee's recording becomes the standard and almost everyone forgets I ever did the song."

Raskin whistled softly, ran the flat of his hand along the side of his jaw. "I see what you mean. But how about the company that recorded your version? Won't they stand behind you?"

"For a while. But when they see what's happening to my side sales-wise and they get the flash from the deejays that everything I touch will get the same treatment, they cool off."

"You mean they let a guy like Marlon kill a valuable property for them?"

The blonde shrugged. "It's like Shannon said. Guys like Marlon make an artist, they can cut her down. Look at it this way: a company ties a lot of money into cutting a side. If they know it's going to get stiffed in advance, you think they're going to worry about what happens to Dinah Reed or anybody else? An A and R man couldn't take the chance, so he either don't assign anything to the artists on Marlon's list or he gives them the scrapings. Either way, you're dead."

"Unbelievable, eh, Raskin?" Hughes grunted. "It would make a good story if—"

"If what?" the blonde wanted to know.

"If we can get anybody to talk. What do you think, Mr. Hughes?"

The city editor exhaled a thick blue cloud of smoke, squinted through it. "How about the trade papers in the field? They done anything about it?"

The girl shook her head.

"I wonder why not?" Raskin scowled.

"For the reason you mentioned," the city editor told him. "I doubt if anyone will open up and talk." He turned to the blonde. "The A and R man at the company that recorded your song. Who's he?"

"Arnie Cohen."

"Think he'd be willing to substantiate what you've told us?"

Dinah considered, shook her head. "I don't think he'd stand up to Marlon. He'd be practically committing suicide in the business."

Hughes nodded. "There you are, Raskin. There's your problem. Everybody knows what's going on, but nobody will talk."

The reporter chewed on the end of his pencil, scowled in concentration. "Then there must be another way to get at it."

"Such as?"

Raskin turned to the girl. "You say the artists have to stay on the right side of the disc jockeys as well as the A and R men. Have you ever given any money to Marlon or any of the others?"

The blonde shook her head. "Christmas presents, personal appearances, stuff like that."

The reporter looked disappointed. "But you couldn't put your finger on any money he received?"

The blonde shook her head.

"What's perking in your head, Sam?" Hughes wanted to know.

"There's more than one way to get at a racketeer like Marlon. Capone found that out. If we could trace some dough that went to him directly that he didn't report ..."

The city editor knocked the dottle out of his pipe into his palm, spilled it into the wastebasket. "Income tax, eh? It would do it. But it would take some proving." His eyes swung to the girl. "You don't know of any instance where Marlon asked for or received any money?" The girl shook her head. "You've never seen Cohen make any payments to him?"

"No." She caught her lower lip between her teeth, worried it. "I did hear one thing about Marlon and Arnie Cohen, though. I heard they were partners."

"In what?"

"A music-publishing firm." She watched while Raskin scribbled the information on his paper. "I couldn't prove it, but I've heard a lot of people say it was true."

Hughes tugged at his nose with thumb and forefinger. "Do you know the name of the firm?"

"Devine Music. Joe Devine is supposed to be running the company. A few years ago he was just another little Poverty Row publisher. But recently he's latched onto a couple of real hot numbers. He's going great."

Hughes looked disappointed. "That's not much to go on."

"Well, almost every big number he's had has been recorded by Rhythm Records," the girl put in. "And they've all had a big spin from Marlon."

Raskin looked up from his paper, pursed his lips. "Could be, Mr. Hughes. Devine gets a number, sends it over to Cohen—"

"Or more likely, Cohen hears it and agrees to record it and suggests that Devine publish it," the girl interrupted. "That's the way it usually happens."

The reporter nodded his head. "That's even better. Then Marlon plays it into the hit class." His gaze darted from the girl to Hughes and back. "They really have it made."

"And Marlon would probably be making a third of the profits," Hughes mused. "Suppose he didn't report those?"

"What can we lose by finding out?" Raskin wanted to know.

The city editor reached out for a telephone. "Get me Al Norman in Treasury Intelligence at the Federal Building, honey." While he waited he drummed on the desk. "You're willing to go all the way with this, Miss Reed?"

The blonde hesitated for a moment, then nodded "All the way."

"Good." He returned his attention to the phone. "Al? Bill Hughes over at the *Standard*. I've run into something that sounds like it might be right up your alley. Real big. There's just one string attached to it—" He grinned as he listened to the man on the other end. "That's right, we want the story first. Is it a deal?" He winked at the girl while the man at the other end argued. "Sorry, Al. No exclusive, no deal. We'll dig it up ourselves." He smiled at the capitulation of the other man. "Good. You know Sam Raskin from my staff? He'll be right over with a young woman. Her story will knock your hat off."

21

Following Dinah Reed's visit to Treasury Intelligence, several months passed with no apparent progress being made. In the beginning she would check regularly with Bill Hughes at the *Standard* to see if there were any developments. Then the calls became less and less frequent as she became convinced that her efforts to get back at the disc jockey had been a dry run.

It was almost four months to the day that Al Norman, the Treasury Intelligence agent, pushed back a pile of accumulated reports that represented months of intensive research and grinned at his partner. Norman had none of the characteristic appearance of a ferret. His moon-shaped, sunburned face was a deep mahogany, and when he smiled, dimples cut deep trenches in his cheeks.

"We've got them, buster," he told his partner. "We've really got 'em. This one will tear the lid off from here to the coast and back." He leaned back in his chair and stretched. "Those bastards have been getting away with murder, and if it hadn't been for that chantoosie they'd still be. But we've got 'em now."

"Take it easy, kid, and don't go off half cocked." Les

Dale, Norman's partner, was an old-timer. He affected a rumpled blue suit, a battered and stained gray fedora. His jaws were in perpetual motion, a toothpick protruding from the corner of his lips. "I went over that Eddie Marlon file pretty close. That character's no pushover."

"You think I don't know it? He's the guy's been giving me the real bad time," Norman grunted. "Matter of fact, even now I don't think we could get an okay to give him a going over on the basis of his returns. They look pretty clean—as far as they go."

"Meaning?"

"They don't go far enough." Norman indicated the pile of memoranda on the corner of his desk. "Have you checked the returns of the various A and R men?"

Dale shook his head. "Not too closely. Anyone in particular?"

"Yeah. Arnie Cohen down at Rhythm Records."

The older man plucked the toothpick from between his teeth, regarded the battered end owlishly. "The one the Reed girl put the finger on? I looked him over." He shrugged. "A big operator."

"Real big," Norman grunted. He burrowed through the pile on the desk, brought up an analysis of Cohen's return. "Shows an income of $175,000 last year." He looked up. "Expenses almost seventy-five grand."

"You got to spend money to make money."

"Yeah, but cross-check his return against Rhythm's corporate return." He underscored an item with his thumbnail. "This boy's been riding heavy on the company swindle sheet, too. What's the extra seventy-five grand for? Petty cash?"

Dale pushed back the fedora, scratched at his scalp. "I thought we were after the disc-jockey syndicate."

"We are."

The older man frowned at him. "So what's with the A and R man kick?"

"Even taking for granted that some of these excessive expense accounts will show up as 'gifts' to the disc jockeys, I've got a hunch there's something else in there that might not be reported."

"Such as?"

"Commissions, profits from a side business." Norman tossed the breakdown onto the pile. "Marlon was smart enough to list gifts and stuff like that that we could trace. But if the blonde was right and he gets a piece of some songs or even a piece of a publishing house, he didn't report that. And that could turn out to be awful expensive."

His partner chewed thoughtfully on the toothpick, walked over, picked up the analysis, ran experienced eyes over the breakdown. "That would mean we've got to persuade Cohen to open up on Marlon."

"Or convince him he's going to take the rap himself. When we spell it out for him, guess which?"

Dale bobbed his head. "I see what you mean." He flipped the toothpick at the wastebasket. "Anything else?"

"Yeah. I had a rundown made on the music firm he's supposed to have a piece of. Devine Music. An interesting picture." He leaned over the desk, flipped through the pile of papers, consulted some penciled figures. "Firm's return shows almost eighty per cent of income written off as advertising and promotion. We did a check on five other firms doing roughly the same volume. Average for advertising and promotion runs less than thirty per cent."

"The extra fifty percent could be Marlon and Cohen, eh?"

Norman nodded. "Could be. But neither of them

shows it as income. Devine Music reports pretty hefty promotion expenses at Rhythm. That probably goes to Cohen and he takes care of Marlon's share."

"That could account for those excessive expense accounts."

"That's what I'm hoping. Because if it is, we've got Marlon, but good." He got up, walked to the hatrack in the corner, lifted off his fedora. "Once we nail him, that syndicate of his will fall apart and the boys will all be blowing whistles trying to get out from under."

"We going some place?"

"Uptown. I have a sudden yen to make conversation with this Devine character. Then, from there we can drop by and say hello to Mr. Cohen. I've got an idea he's going to sing 'Dixie' and this I've got to hear."

The musicians, the pluggers, the would-be song writers, the once-big song writers, and the never-was song writers were clustered in little knots on the sidewalk outside the Brill, all the way down the corridor to the elevator bank when Al Norman and his partner walked in.

They headed for the listing board next to the elevators, checked for the room number of Devine Music. The elevator dropped them at the tenth floor, they walked the length of the corridor to the double frosted-glass doors bearing the information *Devine Music Co.*

The anteroom throbbed with an early-afternoon buzz of activity as they pushed the door open and walked in. Song writers stood, or lounged around, waiting to be summoned to the inner sanctum.

A telephone operator-receptionist sat in a glass booth that faced out on the anteroom. She seemed undisturbed by the hum of activity, leafed through the pages of a movie magazine.

Al Norman walked over to the glassed-in cubicle, rapped on the window with his knuckles. The girl inside turned an annoyed look on him. She slid back a little panel.

"Look, lover," she told him. "You're prettier than the rest but it won't do you no good. Mr. Devine's taking them as they came and you came last."

He dug a little leather holder from his pocket, flipped it open to a gold badge.

"The longer he keeps me waiting, the harder I am to get along with," he told her. "Tell him it's Treasury Intelligence. On his taxes."

The girl's gaze moved quickly from his face to the badge and back. She nodded, slid the panel shut, stuck a plug in a hole and wiggled a key back and forth. While she spoke into the mouthpiece, her eyes never left the T-man's face. She yanked the plug out, slid the partition back. "He'll be right with you."

Les Dale was standing at the far wall, examining a huge case filled with records. A system of interior lighting flooded the case, managed to make the gold record mounted in the center of the case stand out like some precious jewel.

As Al Norman joined his partner, a door to the right opened. A tall, worried-looking man stuck his head out. "Mr. Norman?" He looked around, dismissed the familiar faces that lined the anteroom.

When Norman walked over to him, Devine reached out, shook the T-man's with a moist hand.

"Come in, come in." He led the way into the inner office, ignored the angry shouts of the others, closed the door. Then he walked around the desk, dropped into the upholstered swivel chair. "Maybe I could offer you gentlemen a drink?"

"Not while we're on duty," Norman told him.

"On duty?" Devine's voice quavered. "You make it sound so—so official."

"It is, Mr. Devine. I might as well tell you that we've been investigating your returns. There are some things about them that require explanation."

"My returns?" Devine put his hands to his chest, managed to look shocked. "You don't think I would try to cheat Uncle Sammy?"

"I hope not." Norman pulled a chair close to the desk. "For your sake." He sat down, pulled a sheaf of papers from his inside pocket. "You are sole owner of the Devine Music Co."

Joe Devine licked at his lips, shrugged. "It ain't so much as it looks. I—"

"You're sole owner?"

The man behind the desk rubbed his damp palms together. "Well, I—" He wilted under the direct stare of the T-man. "Not exactly."

Les Dale stuck a fresh toothpick between his teeth. "What's that mean, Mr. Devine?"

The dry wash of the hands became more agitated. "I have a sort of—well, a sort of silent partner."

Al Norman consulted the papers in his hand, frowned. "I don't see any record of him."

Joe Devine worked at a smile, ended with just twitching his lips. "He—he doesn't like to appear. Nothing illegal or shady, you understand," he amended hastily. "It's—well, it's just that somebody might think it was unethical."

"He's in the business?"

Devine's head bobbed miserably. "He's what we call an A and R man. He can get songs recorded and somebody might think—"

The publisher looked from one to the other, got no encouragement. "Well, look, it ain't nothin' I did. I'm just the beard for the operation." He dug a handkerchief from his breast pocket, blotted his forehead. "I'm just a Poverty Row publisher when they make me the proposition." His eyes darted back and forth. "Nobody can blame me."

"This partner of yours. What's his name?"

Devine licked at his lips, seemed to deflate. "Cohen. Arnold Cohen of Rhythm Records."

"I'm glad you're being smart, Mr. Devine. If you had tried to mislead us, it might have been pretty serious for you." Norman returned the papers to his pocket. "We'll need a deposition from you."

The man behind the desk swabbed at his face. "Am I in bad trouble?"

Norman pursed his lips. "You could be if you tried to play tricks on us, but if you co-operate and if your personal returns are in order, I'd say you stand a pretty good chance of walking away from it."

Devine's head bobbed like a cork in a stormy inlet. "I'm with you, mister. Look, I do what I'm told, but if these schlemiels think Joe Devine takes the fall and gets paid off in gold"—he raised his hands, cocked his head—"this strictly ain't for me."

"We're going to ask you to come along with us and we'll want any records or any vouchers you may have to back up your contention that Arnie Cohen has an affiliation with this company."

"I don't have that stuff right in the office—"

Norman scowled at him.

"No, no." Devine shook his head hastily. "No tricks. It's just that all the papers are at my accountant's." He reached for the phone. "A nice boy. My sister's boy. He could meet us at your office."

He punched the button on the side of the phone. "Call Irving, the accountant. Tell him he should meet me at—" He looked inquiringly at the moon-faced man.

"Federal Building. Agent Norman, Treasury Intelligence."

"—at the Federal Building. In the office of Agent Norman of Treasury Intelligence." He wiped his forehead. "Tell him to bring all vouchers on payments to Arnold Cohen and a copy of the partnership papers. Tell him I'm leaving now, I expect him to be there when I get there."

Arnie Cohen sat on the couch in his apartment, his fat dimpled hands resting on his knees. His eyes were almost lost behind the discolored pouches, veiled by the heavily veined lids. He studied the moon-faced man in the upholstered chair opposite him.

"So you got a deposition from Joe Devine? So I'm a silent partner in his operation? It might not sound too good in the trade, but it's not illegal." His voice sounded choked by the heaviness of his jowls.

"We have a statement of your earnings from Devine." Al Norman tapped the sheaf of papers against his palm. "It doesn't jibe with your income-tax return."

The fat man blew his pouty lips in and out. "I didn't get it all," he countered defensively. "Only a part of it was mine."

"We're not interested in that. We're interested in the fact that you failed to report a substantial amount in earnings. Of course, if there's an explanation—"

"I didn't get all that, I tell you. I was just the collection agent for someone else." His stubby fingers played nervously with a huge diamond on the sausage-shaped fourth finger of his right hand. "How can you expect me to report income I didn't get?"

"Who got it?"

Cohen pursed his lips thoughtfully. "Look. How deep am I in?"

Norman looked to his partner, drew a shrug. "It's only a guess, Mr. Cohen, but I'd say pretty deep. Uncle Sam takes it pretty seriously when somebody evades his taxes or conspires with someone to help that someone evade them. It looks to me as if you did a little bit of both."

The fat man shook his head. "It's not the way it looks."

The T-man referred to a notation on the sheaf of papers. "Your expenses are away out of line, for one thing. Away out."

"All A and R men have heavy expenses. You don't know these band leaders, these vocalists—"

"And these disc jockeys?"

Cohen bobbed his head vehemently. "And disc jockeys. It's presents, all the time. Dinners and shows. They even tell you what night is your night to take them and the woman out, where you'll take them and how much you spend."

"These presents? Are they ever cash?"

The little eyes retreated farther behind the discolored lids. "Look, mister, I got to make a living out of this industry. You're asking me to blow the whistle. That I can't do."

Norman shrugged. "Then we have to assume that you knowingly and deliberately falsified your returns, and—"

"What are you saying?" Cohen's eyes snapped wide open in apprehension. "You think I'm crazy? I never fool with the man with the whiskers!" He licked at his overripe lips with a swollen tongue. "Can we make a deal?"

"I don't know that you're in a position to deal, Cohen,"

Norman told him frankly. "If you've been covering for somebody, you did such a good job of it that he's liable to be able to make it stick."

"Arnie Cohen never got any medals for being smart in school, mister, but nobody leaves Arnie holding no bag." He looked from Norman to his partner and back. "You see I get a break and I'll bust open the biggest racket you ever heard of." He lowered his voice, leaned forward. "A disc jockey syndicate all over the country that shakes publishers, record companies, and artists for plenty."

"Why should anybody kick through?"

"You kidding?" The fat man distributed a fine spray of spit in emphasis. "Anybody who can control whether records get a spin or not can control the companies and even pick the artists. I can prove to you one case where a girl who wouldn't play ball was blackballed by the syndicate and couldn't get a company in the business to cut a disc for her." He stabbed a pudgy finger at them. "And only last year she was the hottest thing in the business."

"They have that much power?"

Cohen snorted. "That much power? More. You think the companies cut them in on a new record because they like the way they part their hair? No. Because by playing it over and over they can make even a dog a hit. These guys can kill an established artist and make a freak a best seller. And they're doing it all the time."

"Who's key man in the operation?"

"A little rat named Eddie Marlon."

"You can give us proof, not just conversation?"

Cohen settled back, touched the tips of his fingers across his stomach. "I can blow the lid off the whole mess. Names, places, dates, and amounts."

Norman looked to Les Dale, drew a nod.

"All right. You prove to us you can deliver what you've just promised and I'll put in a word with the Federal D.A. The better your stuff is, the better the word."

The fat man nodded. "Have him at your office and I spill."

Norman walked to the phone, lifted it from its hook, dialed a number. "This is Norman. Have someone from the D.A.'s office there in about half an hour. I'm bringing Arnie Cohen in. He's ready to make a statement."

He listened to the chatter of the party on the other end, nodded. "We're going to make a deal with him in return for a lot of information on a disc-jockey syndicate. From the little I've heard, there's plenty to go on for a series of indictments all over the country."

The receiver chattered back briefly.

"One other thing"—Norman lowered his voice—"have Sam Raskin of the *Standard* there. This is his story and I promised him first crack when it broke." He dropped the receiver back on its hook. "Okay, Cohen, let's go."

The fat man pulled himself off the couch with a grunt, waddled to the closet. He carefully selected a pearl-gray homburg, fitted it to the top of his head.

"You may not know it, but you just made the best damn' deal the law's ever made." He waddled over to join them at the door. "Those bastards have been riding too high anyway. I hope you have enough stenographers ready, because I'm just in the mood to blow the lid off the whole filthy music business."

22

Eddie Marlon got his first intimation of the gathering storm when he came off the air that night. Mike Shannon was standing at the studio door, caught him by the arm as he walked out.

"Eddie, I got to talk to you."

"Not right now, Mike." Eddie shook his hand off. "I've got to see Dickenson on a—"

"Eddie!" There was a note of urgency in Shannon's voice. "They been grilling Joe Devine and Arnie Cohen. All hell's getting ready to blow loose."

Marlon scowled at the other man, noticed for the first time the panic in his eyes. "Who's grilling them?"

"Treasury. I got word from a good contact that Arnie Cohen's getting ready to blow the whistle on the whole setup. You know what that means if he does?"

Marlon stared at the other man for a moment. "Why would he spill? He's in as deep as anybody. He shoots his mouth off and he's finished in—"

"He's finished anyway, don't you get it? They've been shaking down his income-tax returns and he either has to sing or face a nice rap."

The seriousness of the situation began to dawn on the thin man. "Meet me at my place in about an hour. Meantime, keep your ears open and see what you can hear around."

"Where are you going?"

"Up to see John K. Dickenson. I pulled him off a hot spot once. Now it's his turn."

"At your place in an hour." Shannon nodded.

Marlon watched his associate hustle down the hall in the direction of the elevator. When Shannon turned at the far end of the corridor, the thin man headed for the executive elevators. He couldn't conceive that Arnie Cohen would be insane enough to mark finis to his career in the music industry by blowing the whistle, but it still wouldn't hurt to take a few precautions.

The blonde in the outside office of John K. Dickenson's suite greeted him coldly, announced him to Dickenson immediately. There was a short pause before his voice came back through the intercom inviting Marlon in.

Dickenson was sitting behind his desk, fingering a letter opener, when the thin man walked into his office.

"Hello, J. K." Marlon went to the big armchair opposite the desk, dropped into it with a sigh. "You don't seem very happy to see me."

"It's such a rare pleasure. And it's usually so costly I'm not sure that I am." Dickenson dropped the letter opener, swung around, took a bottle and two glasses from the bar. "Too early for a drink?"

"Matter of fact I can use one."

The white-haired man dropped two ice cubes into each glass, poured bourbon over them, pushed one glass across the desk. He watched while Marlon leaned forward, lifted the glass.

"I trust the object of the visit isn't to take over the rest of the available time on the station?" he said.

Marlon grinned glumly. "I've got all I can handle."

Dickenson nodded, settled back. "That's nice." He waited for the thin man to proceed.

"J. K., there may be a little trouble."

The white-haired man offered no comment.

"I just got word that the Treasury Department is beginning to root into the music business."

"I'd say it was about time. But that's strictly a personal opinion."

"Mike Shannon tells me they've had a couple of A and R men down on the grill and they're singing like stage-struck canaries." The thin man held his glass under his nose, sniffed. "They can't account for some of their expense accounts so they're claiming they used the dough for payola."

For the first time Dickenson looked concerned. "Can they prove it?"

Marlon grinned crookedly. "Why don't you ask if it's true?"

"Can they prove it?"

"Not by me."

The white-haired man's eyes narrowed. "Look, Marlon, I haven't interfered with the way you've been operating—"

"I've been making money for you."

Dickenson nodded. "Exactly. You've been making money for us. But if on your own you've got into something, you're strictly on your own."

Marlon swirled the liquor around in his glass, pursed his lips. "Them's harsh words, coming from an employer to his favorite employee."

"Favorite employee? Don't make my stomach turn."

"If you're thinking of throwing me to the wolves, Dickenson, you've got another think coming. If I go down, a lot of people go down with me."

The white-haired man sipped at his glass, raised his eyebrows politely. "That sounds almost like a threat."

"It's no threat, it's a promise."

"Then you think other people have been taking kickbacks from the music people as well as you, or—"

"I don't mean that," Marlon snarled. "I covered up

for you once, and I'm expecting you to cover up for me now."

Dickenson smiled bleakly, shook his head from side to side. "I paid that debt, remember? We made a deal and I lived up to my part of it. I don't think you have any choice but to live up to your part of it."

Marlon stared at him with stricken eyes. "You'd walk away from it? I kept you out of jail and if you think I won't scream to high heaven—"

"About what?"

"About Jo Leary, that's what."

Dickenson looked politely interested. "Jo Leary?"

"Maybe you've forgotten about it, but the papers won't. Not after I remind them. You're still good copy, Dickenson, and the tabs will have a picnic taking a stuffed shirt like you apart."

"A few years ago you might have had a bargaining point, Marlon, but that was a few years ago."

"You're still as good copy now as you were then."

Dickenson considered it, nodded. "But Jo Leary isn't. You see, she met a man on that trip around the world I financed. They're married. You might have a lot of difficulty persuading her to testify."

"She'll testify."

The white-haired man regarded him thoughtfully for a moment. "It mightn't do you very much good if she did." He got up from behind the desk, took a small key ring from the upper drawer. He selected one key from it, walked to an oil painting on the far wall. Behind it was a small safe that opened to the key. He fumbled in the interior for a moment, came back with an envelope. He took several folded papers from the envelope, satisfied himself they were the sheets he wanted.

"You don't seem to have very much respect for my

good judgment, Marlon." He smiled. "Naturally, before Jo took her trip, we had a little session with my attorney." He tapped the folded sheets against the palm of his hand. "These are photostats. One is her statement concerning the assault and battery you committed on her in the Denton Apartments."

"You couldn't make that stick," Marlon roared.

The white-haired man held up his hand. "Just a minute. I also have here the statements, both sworn to, of course, of the clerk and the switchboard operator at a place called"—he hesitated, consulted one of the sheets of paper—"the Spotlight Residence Club. They refer to a number of visits you made to Miss Leary when she lived at that establishment." He looked up. "Prior to the date of the attack." He held the sheets out. "Would you like to see them?"

The color had drained from Marlon's face. He snatched the sheets from the older man's hand, read through them, swore under his breath. "You can't figure these will stand up. Otherwise, why have you been stringing along with me on the program, giving me everything I want?"

Dickenson shrugged. "You said it yourself. You've been making money for the station. A lot of money."

"But you'd throw me to the wolves?"

Dickenson raised his hands, palms upward. "Would I have any choice?"

Marlon swore at him, ripped the sheets of papers across, kept tearing them until they were small fragments. Dickenson watched, without change of expression.

"As I explained to you," the white-haired man told him. "Those are photostats. The originals, of course, are in the hands of my attorney."

Marlon got up, stamped to the door. He stopped with

his hand on the knob. "Don't sell me short, Dickenson. I'll beat this rap and I'll make you sorry you didn't help me when I needed it."

"Come in any time. Always glad to see you." Dickenson turned his back, walked to the safe, locked it and made a production of straightening the oil painting over it. When he turned around, Marlon had left.

23

Mike Shannon was pacing the living-room when Eddie Marlon let himself into the apartment with his key. An unlighted cigar drooped from the corner of Shannon's mouth, a half-consumed glass of Scotch sat forgotten on the coffee table. He looked to Marlon eagerly as the thin man came in.

"Well?"

Marlon shook his head. "I thought Dickenson would stand up but the sonofabitch turned me down. We're strictly on our own." He tossed his hat at the couch, walked into the kitchenette, and poured himself a stiff shot of bourbon. "How about you?"

"Big trouble. Real big." Shannon resumed pacing the room. "Word's out that Cohen is really blowing the whistle." He stopped, scowled at Marlon. "Your little playmate Joe Devine's been shooting off at the mouth, too."

"The dirty ungrateful louse. How about that? You take a shoestringer like that, put him in the bucks, and what thanks do you get?" He dropped onto the couch, squinted at the shiny tips of his shoes. "When this is all over, I'll crucify that fat bastard of a Cohen."

"If he don't do it to us first," Shannon mumbled. "You know how this whole kick got started?"

Marlon shook his head.

"Dinah Reed. She went around screaming that you were persecuting her. Some newspaper guy with the hots for those knockers of hers takes her up to the Treasury guys. They smell a take and start shaking."

"Don't worry. They haven't got a thing on us."

"You sure?"

The thin man shrugged. "Of course I'm sure. You think I didn't figure maybe the day would come someone would blow the whistle?" He sipped at his drink. "They got my income-tax returns. Let them show me I got any more than I declared. They haven't got a thing on me. "

"You could fool me. You look like you're getting ready to shake yourself apart." Shannon pulled the cigar from between his teeth, bounced it off the floor. "They sure as hell haven't got anything on me. I didn't get any of the loot from that operation."

"I'm not worried as much as I am mad." Marlon tossed off the drink, got up and stalked to the phone. He picked up the receiver. "I want to call Chicago person to person. Dick Lobe at Monroe 6-8099. My number?" He squinted at the dial. "Plaza 3-4598. Yeah, I'll hold on." He placed his palm over the mouthpiece. "Freshen that drink of mine, will you, Mike?"

Shannon picked up the glass, disappeared into the kitchenette. He came back with three fingers of bourbon, handed it to the man on the phone.

"That's right, operator. Dick Lobe."

"Who's calling from New York?" the operator's metallic voice wanted to know.

"Eddie Marlon."

There was a pause, then the familiar voice of the Chicago disc jockey came through. "Marlon? What the hell's going on?" he asked without preliminaries. "I just got a paper to appear at the Federal Building out here in the morning."

"A couple of A and R men here got picked up on their returns and they're blowing the whistle on gifts to deejays. Sit tight, they haven't got a thing on us."

"That's not the way I hear it. I been through to Ed Decker, on *Radio Confidential*. He says all hell's going to break loose."

"Look, don't get your bowels in an uproar. If we stick together, they can't do a thing—"

Lobe's snort came across the wires. "What's the 'stick together' routine. They're not after us, they're after you, buster."

"Me?"

"Yeah. You didn't cut us schnooks in on that music-publishing deal or a lot of other personal graft you were pulling. That's what they're after, Ed says. Not a hunch of petty-larceny expense accounts."

"Wait a minute, Lobe—"

"For all I know, they got your wire tapped right now. And if they have, I'm on record right now. I have no part of you or anything you're mixed up in. I got sucked into an organization of disc jockeys and if the organization was used for anything illegal, I had no part—"

Marlon slammed the receiver back on its hook. He swore at it long and fervently. "They're bailing out." He swung on Shannon. "You talk to anybody down at *Radio Confidential?*"

Shannon nodded. "Ed Decker."

The little man strode to the coffee table, snagged a cigarette, lighted it and smoked with short, angry puffs. "The word's out and they're all running for cover. If Lobe's been subpoenaed, so have the rest." He reached down, snubbed out the cigarette. "I got to reach somebody to turn this heat off."

"Who?"

Marlon's eyes narrowed. "Endres. Johnny Endres. He's got plenty of lines that feed right into Washington. He could do it. He better do it." He reached for his personal telephone directory, flipped through it, ran his finger down the page to a name and number. He picked up the phone, decided against it, replaced it on the hook. "Maybe Lobe's right. Maybe they got a bug on my wire. I'd better use the pay phone in the lobby." He picked up another cigarette, lighted it, took a deep drag. "What time is it?"

Shannon consulted the watch on his wrist. "Seven-thirty."

"He won't be at the club until late." He started pacing the room, took another drag on the cigarette and crushed out the half-smoked butt. By nine, the bowl was filled with two and two-and-a-half-inch butts.

"How come they've served all the others and haven't served me yet?" he demanded suddenly. "How come?"

"Maybe they're waiting until they have enough on you for an airtight case, and—"

Marlon stared at him. "You! How come you haven't been served?"

"Me?" Shannon stared at him for a minute. "Maybe they been trying to reach me. I been here all evening and at the studio all afternoon."

The thin man pointed to the phone. "Call your place. See if anybody's been there looking for you."

Obediently, Shannon crossed to the phone, dialed his own number. After a moment he was connected. He spoke in a low tone, nodded and hung up. "There's been a guy looking for me three or four times today," he said. "The super says he looks like a process server."

Agent Al Norman sat back in his desk chair, stared

at the cracks in the ceiling, his hands folded in his lap. He was tired after a long day of deposition taking, disappointed with some of the results.

"You might have known Marlon wouldn't be stupid enough to take the money openly and not declare it," Les Dale drawled. "Matter of fact, a smart lawyer could make monkeys out of us. There's nobody to testify that he ever took a dime—at least not a dime he hasn't declared."

Norman rolled his eyes down from the ceiling. "They gave it to his stooge. What's his name?"

"Mike Shannon?"

"Yeah. They gave him the dough. Both Devine and Cohen will swear to that."

Dale nodded. "Sure, if you're looking for a case against the bagman, you've probably got it made. But what happened to it after Shannon got it? It hasn't shown up in any of Marlon's savings accounts."

"A safe-deposit box."

"That makes it sound nice and simple. Now all we have to do is get a court order to open every safe-deposit box in the city. Or maybe the state."

Norman growled under his breath. "How about picking up Shannon? Maybe he knows where Marlon's been stashing the loot."

Dale considered it, shrugged. "We can pick him up, but if this Marlon's half as smart as he sounds, he isn't confiding where he's keeping his loot to anyone."

"If we throw enough of a scare into Shannon he'll tell us everything he knows. Out of it we may get a lead."

"How big a scare are you planning to throw into him?"

"The works. We can trace the money from both Devine and Cohen to him. It'll be up to him to prove that he passed it along to Marlon."

Dale pursed his lips, scratched at his head. "It might work, at that." He checked his watch. "Want to pick him up tonight?"

"Might as well. I'd like to get this thing wrapped up as soon as possible. By now Marlon must know what's going on and he's probably busy covering up his tracks. The longer he has to do it, the better the job he'll do."

Dale checked with the front office by phone. "We have a paper out for Shannon. Hasn't been served yet."

"Means he hasn't gone back to his place. He's either with Marlon or at his girl's place." He referred to the sheet in front of him. "Her name's Jackie Martin. Lives on 35th Street. Want a pickup on him at her address and at Marlon's?"

The man in the rumpled blue suit nodded. "He'll be at one or the other."

24

Eddie Marlon was unaware that Mike Shannon had been picked up outside the apartment building on his way to Jackie Martin's. Three times during the next two hours he went down to the lobby to try to reach Johnny Endres from the pay phone located there. It was almost midnight when he finally got through to Endres.

"This is Eddie Marlon. I've got to see you."

Endres's voice was cold. "Where are you calling from?"

"A pay phone in the lobby of my apartment house." The perspiration was beginning to dampen his hairline in the close confines of the booth. He blotted it with a wadded handkerchief. "I want to talk to you."

"Not over the telephone," Endres snapped at him.

"Where?"

Endres sighed. "Can't it wait?"

"No. I'm in trouble. I need some help."

There was a brief pause. "My car will call for you. Be ready in about twenty minutes. Follow exactly the instructions of the man who calls."

Marlon said he would, dropped the receiver on its hook. For the first time he was beginning to be scared. He pushed his way out of the booth, ascended in the elevator to his floor, chain smoked until the buzzer to his door sounded. He opened it. A man in a light-colored belted raincoat and a dark fedora entered. He looked around. "You're alone?"

Marlon nodded.

The newcomer started stripping off the coat and held out the hat. "You'll wear this hat and my coat. The car is parked at the entrance. A black Cadillac with its lights burning. You will walk directly to it and get in."

"Why all the cloak and dagger?"

"The building is probably being watched. Mr. Endres would not like you to be followed to his place." He watched while Marlon slipped into the coat, pulled the hat low over his face.

"Okay?" Marlon asked.

The other man studied him critically, nodded. "When you go out, don't walk too slowly or they may recognize you, nor fast enough to call attention to yourself. They saw me come in, they will take for granted they are seeing me leave."

Marlon nodded. He opened the door, walked down the hallway to the elevator. In the lobby he tugged the brim of the hat down, headed for the street. He could see the lights of the Cadillac to the left of the entrance. He cut across the sidewalk to the car, opened the door, and slid into the back seat. The driver, without a word, swung the car out into a lane of traffic.

Johnny Endres lived in a turreted old stone building above the Jersey Palisades just north of the George Washington Bridge. The car slowed down for an okay as it approached a pair of huge, wrought-iron gates. At a signal from the gateman, the car entered, followed the winding road to the house.

A man in livery, whose bulking shoulders made him appear more suitable for the role of bodyguard than butler, opened the door. When he took Marlon's coat, he expertly fanned him, made certain he was not armed. Then, without explanation, he indicated a door to the right of the main hall.

The room beyond was half den, half library. It was a big room with knotty-pine paneling and Indian rugs. A huge picture window took up most of one wall, its colorful curtains drawn, cutting off what in the daytime was a panoramic view of the Hudson.

Johnny Endres was sprawled comfortably in an armchair. He waved to Eddie Marlon as the thin man walked in.

"I don't usually transact business in my home," he explained, "but you sounded urgent."

"You've heard about the investigation?"

Endres pursed his lips, studied his fingernails. "I've heard something about it." He looked up. "It sounds like you got a little greedy." He returned his gaze to his nails. "That's bad."

"Look, Johnny, I need help. I know you have contacts ..."

The man in the chair polished his nails with the ball of his thumb, didn't look up. "I have a lot of contacts," he agreed amiably. "But what does that have to do with you?"

"I figured maybe you'd put in a word for me, and—"

Endres looked up. "Why should I?"

"I might be in a position to help you some day."

The man in the chair pursed his lips, considered it, then shook his head. "I don't think so." He settled back against the cushions, stared at the thin man. "I think your days of being useful to anybody are over. The best advice I can give you is to cop a plea, pay your fine, and take your chances."

"I'm not ready to cop a plea or take my chances."

Endres studied him curiously. "You sound tough."

"Look, I'm not the only one who's been on the take, Endres. Why should I take all the rap? We're all in this—"

"We're all in what?"

"You know damn' well what I'm talking about. If you think I'm going to take the fall alone for shaking these A and R men, you're nuts. Some of that money came over this way. Plenty of it."

Endres pursed his lips thoughtfully, touched the tips of his fingers together, his elbows resting on the arms of the chair. "You mean you're telling me that I either help bail you out or you'll pull me in with you?"

"You're saying that. Not me."

"Why would any of the A and R men pass me any money?"

Marlon grinned bleakly, humorlessly. "Because you're the baby who can spot their discs on the jukes. You told me yourself you ran the juke-box concessions."

Endres nodded his head. "So I did. And you've got it figured we're all in it together and it's up to me to bail us all out. How?"

"Who's stirring up the whole storm? There's only

one guy. Cohen."

"And if Cohen could be persuaded to shut his mouth, we'd all be in the clear." Endres considered it, nodded. "Sounds logical."

"None of the other A and R men would open their mouths if anything happened to Cohen. They'd be scared to," Marlon warmed to his subject. "You don't have to kill him, just throw the fear of God into him."

"And that's what you came all the way over here to tell me?"

Some of the enthusiasm drained out of Marlon; the sound of the cold voice of the man in the chair left a hollow feeling in his stomach. "It was something I couldn't discuss over the phone."

Endres nodded amiably. "I'm glad you didn't." He reached over, pressed a buzzer on the ornate end table at his elbow. "How are you and Tony DeSales getting along these days?"

Marlon shrugged. "You put him in line, he hasn't got out."

The man in the chair managed a smile. "Good." He looked up as the door opened and the light-haired man who had first brought Marlon to him came in. "Have DeSales come here for a minute."

A moment later the crooner pushed open the door. Tonight he was wearing a heavily padded blue-checked sports jacket, a cream-colored sports shirt and navy blue slacks. His hair was carefully piled on top of his head in thickly oiled curls, the sides plastered against his skull above the ears.

"Close the door, Tony," Endres told him. Then, "Your friend here is in trouble. The T-men are after him. He wants us to use a little persuasion to shut up an A and R man who's blowing the whistle. What do you think?"

"I think we ought to let the bastard get what's coming to him."

Endres glanced briefly at Marlon. "He has the idea that if he goes on the griddle for shaking the A and R men for spins on his show, he might make a deal and put the finger on the juke-box owners for spotting certain records and building certain artists."

"I always told you he was a rat, Mr. Endres."

The man in the chair nodded. "Yes, you did." He reached for a cigarette, stuck it in the corner of his mouth. "I don't think there's very much I can do for you, Marlon." He snapped on a tiny lighter, studied the flame. "After all, what's so tough about it? You haven't killed a man"—he moved his gaze from the flame to the thin man—"and you haven't been killed yet."

"You're calling my bluff. Is that it?"

Endres touched the flame to the cigarette, drew a deep breath, exhaled. "See that he gets home, Tony." He leaned his head back against the cushion, seemed to go to sleep.

"Let's go, Marlon." The singer nodded at the door. "I'll see that you get home." He led the way from the den to the outer hall. While Marlon was shrugging into the belted coat, the crooner whispered to the uniformed butler.

The butler nodded, looked from DeSales to the disc jockey. "The car will be right around. If you'd care to wait outside—"

"We'll wait in here. Have them blow the horn when they're ready," DeSales instructed. When the butler had retreated in the direction of backstairs, Tony walked over to where Marlon stood. "You're not very bright, threatening Mr. Endres. He's very narrow-minded about things like that."

Marlon fumbled through the pockets of the raincoat, brought out a pack of cigarettes. He held it out to the singer, who shook his head.

"Bad for my throat."

Marlon grunted, stuck one in his mouth, lighted it. He was almost finished with it when the car outside honked. DeSales led the way through the door to the steps, held the car door for Marlon. There was another man in the back seat, a man who, in profile, looked very much like the butler.

Marlon started to draw back, was shoved into the back seat by DeSales who slid in alongside him. The big car roared, headed for the state road that led south toward the marshes.

25

Mike Shannon sat on a straight-backed wooden chair in Al Norman's office in the Treasury Building and stared with apprehensive eyes at the man behind the desk. "You guys must be kidding me." His eyes jumped from Norman to his partner. "I never got all that dough."

"We just laid it out for you Shannon. We have sworn statements from both Joe Devine and Arnold Cohen that they paid large sums in cash to you."

"For what? I couldn't do them nothing. I couldn't guarantee a spin on their music. That's Eddie Marlon's show, not mine."

"But they gave you money?"

"Sure. But for Eddie, not me." His eyes pleaded for belief. "I was just the bagman. None of the dough stuck to me—except my cut on what the A and R men paid for spins."

"That in your return?"

"Sure. I don't fool around with no income taxes."

Norman and Dale exchanged glances. "How much would you say it amounted to last year?"

"My share?"

Norman nodded.

"I got twenty-five per cent. I figure it ran to about ten, twelve grand last year."

Norman got up, walked to a filing cabinet, flipped through a bunch of folders, selected one, and opened it. "What did Rhythm Records pay you last year, Shannon?"

"About seventy-five hundred."

"And you declared an income of about sixteen thousand." He looked over to his partner. "That's not bad. If that was his total income."

Shannon bobbed his head. "It was. It was."

Norman looked thoughtful, replaced the file. "In that case you've got no problem." He slammed the door shut. "If."

"If what?"

"If you can account for the disposition of roughly $40,000 from other sources." He walked back to his desk. "If you can't you're in trouble."

"What kind of other sources? I get twenty-five per cent from Marlon and a salary from Rhythm. They're both reported. You said so yourself."

"The money from Devine and Cohen?"

"I already told you"—Shannon's face was beginning to gleam wetly—"that was Eddie's. That was the old payola. That was his publishing-company cut. That wasn't for me."

"I believe you, but that's not enough."

"What more can I do?" Shannon pleaded. "I took the money, gave it to Eddie. Ask Cohen, ask Devine. They got no reason to give me any money."

Norman nodded. "You're in a spot, Shannon"—he managed to get a sympathetic note into his voice—"a spot Eddie Marlon put you in deliberately, and he's not going to help you get off it."

Shannon's eyes darted from Norman to his partner and back. "Why would he do that?"

"Because if it's a matter of you or him, guess who?"

Shannon wiped the beaded perspiration off his upper lip with the back of his hand. "You're not getting to me, mister."

Dale broke in. "Let me try to lay it out, Al." He turned to Shannon. "Here's a guy taking a pay-off. He uses a bagman, doesn't take a cent himself. Okay, it blows up. Who's to testify they gave him a dime? Cohen? Devine? Any of the others he shook?" He wagged his head. "All they can say is it was intended for Marlon. But it was you they gave it to."

"But I gave it to him. I'll testify."

"Anybody see you give it to him?"

Shannon shook his head.

"So it's just your word against his."

"Eddie wouldn't do this to me," Shannon protested.

"He's already done it. Why do you think we haven't picked him up yet?" Norman leaned across the desk. "Because we've gone over him with a fine-tooth comb and he's clean." He picked up a paper covered with figures. "He's even listed gifts he got from the A and R men last Christmas." He slammed the sheet back on the desk. "As a matter of fact it's only your admission that you got the money from Cohen that takes him off the hook." He leaned back wearily. "You've been a bit of a schnook, Shannon. And it could get expensive for you."

"The rat. Jackie always said he was a rat, but me,

I—" He broke off. "Wait a minute. I just remembered something. Can I make a call?"

"What about?"

"You want some proof that I passed the money along to Eddie? Right. I think maybe I can get it for you."

Dale flashed a significant glance at his partner. "A witness?"

"Yeah. I think so."

"Why don't we go see him instead of calling?"

"It's a her." He swabbed at his wet forehead. "Her name's Jackie Martin. She's in the line at Harry & Charley's."

Norman consulted his wristwatch. "We can get up to 52nd Street in time for the last show. That way nobody could accuse you of having primed the witness. Okay?"

Shannon bobbed his head uncertainly, licked at his lips. "She's an awful dumb broad. I just hope she remembers."

Most of the tables were still filled at Harry & Charley's when they walked in. A pert little hat-check girl greeted Mike Shannon, eyed his companions with interest.

"Jackie go out, Queenie?" Shannon asked.

"Just for a sandwich after the early show. She's back. Want me to get her out for you?"

"Yeah."

She eyed the two men with him. "Alone?"

"Yeah. Alone." His eyes darted around the club, spotted an isolated table against the back wall. "We'll be over against the wall." He passed a folded bill to her. "Thanks, Queenie."

Shannon and the two T-men threaded their way through the closely set tables, headed for the empty in the back. They ordered drinks, settled back to watch. The place was a babel tonight with out-of-town buyers whooping it up noisily, with waiters clanking silverware and dishes, rushing their orders to have them out of the way before the last show.

Jackie Martin came out from backstage, stood for a moment peering into the dimness of the club, then headed for where they sat. She had already applied her make-up, her lips gleamed a black-red, her eyelashes were beaded with mascara. "Hi, Mike," she greeted Shannon. Her eyes flicked incuriously over the others. "You said you wouldn't be seeing me until after the last show. I wasn't expecting you."

"Sit down, honey," Shannon told her nervously. "I want you to remember something. It's sort of a bet." He licked his lips. "You ever see me with a lot of money?"

The showgirl wrinkled her forehead. "You're always well-heeled, Mike. I never had no complaints—"

He shook his head impatiently. "Important money. Money that didn't belong to me?"

She looked at Norman and Dale with hostile eyes. "What is this, are these guys cops?"

Shannon caught her hand. "Will you concentrate? Did you ever see me with a lot of money I said wasn't mine?"

"The time at my place you mean?"

Shannon sank back, swabbed at his cheeks. "Tell them about it."

"What's to tell?"

Shannon held his face with his hands. "Don't go coy on us now, baby. So I spent the night at your place. They're not interested in that. Tell them about the money."

Jackie reached for the pack of cigarettes on the table,

placed one carefully between her lips so as not to smear the lipstick. "Don't say it like that, like it happens all the time." She bent over, accepted a light from Norman. "Mike got himself as tight as a coot and we had to put him to bed in my place. On the couch, of course."

The T-man blew out the match, nodded for her to continue.

"Dotty was out with Marlon and didn't get in until pretty late. By the time they got home I was sound asleep and Mike was snoring like a seal. Out cold." She carefully detached the cigarette from her lips, studied the carmined end. "The next morning, he looked like he had been dragged through a keyhole. He could hardly get his socks on."

"Get to the money, baby," Shannon pleaded.

"I am," she protested sulkily. "You got to let me tell it my way. I don't want these men thinking—"

"Oh, hell, baby, it's all right. We're going to get married anyhow."

The girl brightened. "We are? When?"

"We'll settle that later. Now before I get too old to enjoy it, finish the story."

"Wait'll I tell Dotty," Jackie exulted.

"The money?" Norman asked patiently.

"Well, like I said, Mike was in no shape for anything. He managed to get dressed and washed, but when he picked up his coat, he picked it up upside down and everything spilled out of his pockets. I knew his eyeballs would fall out if he bent over, so I picked it up for him. There was an envelope. About that thick." She held her thumb and forefinger a half inch apart. "It had Mike's company's name printed in the corner."

"Rhythm Records?" Dale asked.

She nodded. "It wasn't sealed and when it fell, a lot

of money spilled halfway out of it. A helluva lot."

"Go on."

"I tried to count it, but Mike grabbed it away from me. I know there was a couple of thousand in it. Mostly hundreds," she looked to Shannon, got no encouragement. "Mike was real sore at me, said it wasn't his money, that I had no right snooping."

"Did he say whose money it was?"

"Marlon's. He said he picked it up for him."

Norman looked over at his partner, drew a shake of the head. "No more than that?" he asked, disappointment evident in his voice.

The girl shook her head. "No. Mike just took the envelope and sealed it. He wrote Marlon's name on it."

"Go on," Shannon pleaded, "go on."

"That's all, honey. You left it with the desk clerk at Marlon's apartment. I never saw it again."

Shannon slumped in his chair. He dabbed weakly at his forehead. "That it, fellows?"

Norman grinned at him. "I think that's it, Shannon. You're a very lucky guy." He turned to Dale. "What do you think, Les?"

"I think a session with the desk clerk is in order. He'll probably have a record of the package being left and will testify to the delivery to Marlon."

"Mind if I ask a question?" the girl interrupted.

"Go ahead."

"What's this all about?"

Norman grinned. "You just saved your boy friend a nice stretch in a Federal pen."

"Yeah," Shannon groaned, "and in the process it looks like I signed up for a life sentence."

26

Eddie Marlon sat between Tony DeSales and the heavy-shouldered man on his right, watched the scenery go barreling past the windows of the car with growing nervousness.

"How come we're not going back the way we came? Over the George Washington Bridge?" he demanded.

"You're a real hot character tonight, Marlon," De-Sales grinned. "We wouldn't want any of your fans following you. T-men for instance."

When the car swung off the highway and started meandering toward the marshes, Marlon tried to pull out of his seat, got yanked back roughly by the man on his right.

"What are you guys trying to pull?" he wanted to know.

"Stop worrying!" DeSales's jacketed teeth gleamed whitely in the dimness of the car. "Like Mr. Endres says, you haven't killed anyone and you haven't been killed. I'd say you were a pretty lucky fellow."

The car swung onto a rutted dirt road, bumped along for a moment, then came to a stop at a traffic barrier. Beyond it, the ground fell away to a marsh. The man on Marlon's right pushed open the door, stepped out.

"Okay, pal, this is the end of the line," DeSales said. "We got a message for you. Special delivery."

"I'm not getting out," Marlon panted. He tried to squeeze back against the cushions.

The heavy-shouldered man shoved his face into the car, his thick lips grinning in anticipation. He reached in, caught Marlon by the front of his coat, dragged him whimpering out of the car.

"You're crazy. You can't get away with this. They know where I went. They'll get Endres for this, they'll—"

The man with the heavy shoulders brought up a ham-like fist, sank it in the disc jockey's midsection. The air wheezed out of his lungs like a punctured balloon. Before he could slump to the ground, the big man caught him, set him up for another punishing body blow. Marlon's knees folded, he hit the ground face first.

"Don't mark up the face too much," DeSales cautioned the big man. "Just make sure he knows that Mr. Endres don't like bigmouths. When the Feds question him we want him to remember what could have happened."

The bruiser nodded, reached down and caught Marlon by the collar. He yanked him to his feet, propped him against the fender of the Cadillac. Marlon was moaning softly. He was no longer dapper. The thin, purple lips were now blue, the eyes watery, and the carefully combed hair hung down into his face. He was sick. His head rolled uncontrollably from side to side.

DeSales laughed, nodded for the big man to hit him again.

He slammed Marlon across the mouth with the flat of his hand. The disc jockey's head snapped back, a thin stream of blood ran from the corner of his mouth.

"Another one in the mouth to remind him not to be so free with it."

The big man back-handed Marlon again, draped him over the fender. He slid slowly down the fender, hit the ground and rolled over onto his face.

DeSales walked over to where he lay, kicked him in the side. He kept kicking until Marlon stirred, groaned.

DeSales reached down, sank his fingers in the disc jockey's hair, pulled his head up. "Getting the idea, bigmouth?"

Marlon seemed to be having difficulty focusing his eyes. Blood ran from the corner of his mouth. He tried to talk, couldn't.

"How about that?" DeSales chuckled. "A disc jockey—and with nothing to say!"

27

At first it sounded like the peal of thunder. Then it leveled off to a steady beat of a machine gun. Marty Allen opened one bleary eye, decided it was only someone trying to knock down the door to his apartment.

The clock on the night table between the beds showed almost four, the light spilling in under the drawn shade set it as a.m. In the other twin bed, his redheaded wife was struggling to her elbow.

"Who's that, Marty?" she demanded sleepily.

Allen shook his head, slid his feet from under the covers, reached for his robe. "Someone in a hurry sounds like." He fumbled under the bed for slippers. "Keep your pants on. I'm coming."

The pounding stopped. Allen shuffled across the bedroom, through the large living-room toward the door. He left the chain on, opened the door. For a moment he had difficulty in recognizing the battered face of the man in the hall.

"It's me, Allen. Eddie Marlon. Can I come in?" Pink-tinged bubbles formed and broke at the corners of his battered lips.

Allen surveyed the damage to the other man's face,

whistled softly. He unhooked the chain.

"Who is it?" Ann wanted to know.

"Eddie Marlon. Or what's left of him." Allen stepped aside, watched the disc jockey totter to a chair.

"What happened to him?" the girl asked.

"Looks like he just dropped a decision to a buzz saw." Allen replaced the chain on the door, walked over to where Marlon sat. "Can you use a drink, kid?"

The disc jockey nodded, drew the back of his hand across his battered lips. He waited until Allen had poured some liquor in a glass, handed it to him. "Thanks."

"What happened to you?" Allen wanted to know.

"Johnny Endres. A couple of his hoods went to work on me." He took a swallow from the glass, winced as the liquor bit into the rawness of his lips.

"Still making friends and influencing people, eh, Marlon?" Ann walked over to the end table, helped herself to a cigarette. "How long did you figure you could keep on kicking people in the face before they started kicking back?"

"You know Treasury Intelligence is looking for you, kid?" Allen asked.

The man in the chair nodded. "That's why I went to Endres. I figured he could take the heat off."

"Why did you come here?" the redhead wanted to know. She touched a match to her cigarette, blew twin streams of smoke from her nostrils.

"I had to go some place. There was no other place to go." He drained his glass, set it down. "They're all taking a run-out. Dickenson, Cohen, Devine."

"What did you expect them to do? Take the rap for you?"

"I'm not taking any rap. They can't prove a thing," Marlon snarled. "Not a thing."

"You hope," the girl snorted.

"Wait a minute, Annie," Allen put in, "he's had a bad night. Look, kid, I guess you haven't heard about Shannon?"

Marlon looked from Allen to the girl and back. "What about Shannon?"

"He spilled the works. I got the flash from Dickenson. Shannon has pinned you right to a wad of dough from Cohen."

Marlon's jaw sagged. "Why the dirty rat! After all I did for him."

Ann grinned bleakly, shook her head. "You never did a thing for anybody in your life. You just did things to people. Shannon would have stood up, but when he found out you were trying to outsmart him and leave him holding the bag, he got out from under."

"Look, Marty, you got to help me. Go to Dickenson. He'll listen to you. Get him to stand behind me!"

"It's too late for that, kid. Once the cork was out of the bottle, they all started spilling. You know what started this whole thing, kid? Trying to run Dinah Reed out of the business."

"It wasn't just me. Lobe out in Chicago and Michaels on the Coast are just as—"

"They're bailing out. You're getting top billing. It's your show."

"Help me, Marty. Don't let them throw me to the wolves."

"Help you?" There was a note of disbelief in Ann's voice. "You really have the nerve to expect Marty even to lift a finger after what you did to him?"

"I never meant to hurt him."

"You never meant to hurt him. You just elbowed him out of the picture. And after he gave you your start. You turned the business he grew up in into a filthy racket and you used your power to wreck anybody who got in your way. And now you expect him to help you?"

"Look, Marty, I know I've been a heel. I went crazy with my own importance. Okay, so I was wrong. But I'm asking you to help me."

"Even if I would, kid, there's not a helluva lot I can do. The man with the whiskers is tearing the payola racket out by the roots, and from where he sits, you're it."

"What can I do?"

Allen shrugged. "Get a lawyer and take your rap."

"I won't do it. It'd take every cent I have. They can't do that to me, Marty. It ain't fair after the way I worked to get where I am."

Ann shook her head. "How do you like that? They can't do this to Eddie Marlon. He still believes that." She snubbed out her cigarette, walked over to where Marty stood. "I've got a flash for you, Marlon. They've already done it. You're finished. And it's the best thing that could happen to this business."

"Don't you believe it," Marlon snapped. "I'm not through. I did a lot for the music business and they can't—"

"You couldn't even get yourself arrested in it any more, kid," Marty told him sympathetically. "There's a big clean-up coming. Even if you duck a prison term, there's no place left in the industry for the kind of shake you boys have been pulling. All of the stations are working together to clean up the mess. It'll take a long time."

"I made the station money, didn't I?"

Allen shrugged. "Even money can get too expensive when you have to do things like that to get it."

Somewhere an alarm clock shrilled. Ann glanced at

the clock over the fireplace. "I guess it's time to start getting ready, Marty. Almost four-thirty."

Marlon stared at them, realization dawning in his face.

"Four-thirty? Why are you getting up at four-thirty?"

"I guess I forgot to tell you, kid. I'm moving back into the six o'clock slot like in the old days. I'll be taking over the rest of your shows until we can cut down the number of hours skedded for disc shows. I think I'll just keep the early morning and the three-to-five segment. You don't mind if I start getting dressed? I'll want to drop by Murph's for a cup of coffee before I get started."

"You'd better hurry, Marty, if you're going to shave."

Allen grinned at his wife. "You keep forgetting I don't have to fly a desk anymore. From now on, I shave during the news at seven-thirty. That gives me fifteen minutes more to sleep." He turned and stared at Marlon. "Incidentally, if you're smart you'll head for the Federal Building and give yourself up. And it would give a scoop for the seven-thirty news."

THE END

FRANK KANE BIBLIOGRAPHY (1912-1968)

NOVELS

JOHNNY LIDDELL SERIES
About Face (1947; reprinted as Death About Face, 1948; The Fatal Foursome, 1958)
Green Light for Death (1949)
Slay Ride (1950)
Bullet Proof (1951)
Dead Weight (1951)
Bare Trap (1952)
Poisons Unknown (1953)
Grave Danger (1954)
Red Hot Ice (1955)
Johnny Liddell's Morgue (1956; stories)
A Real Gone Guy (1956)
Trigger Mortis (1958)
A Short Bier (1960)
Time to Prey (1960)
Due or Die (1961)
The Mourning After (1961)
Stacked Deck (1961; stories)
Crime of Their Life (1962)
Dead Rite (1962)
Hearse Class Male (1963)
Johnny Come Lately (1963)
Ring-a-Ding Ding (1963)
Barely Seen (1964)
Fatal Undertaking (1964)
Final Curtain (1964)
The Guilt-Edged Frame (1964)
Espirt de Corpse (1965)

Two to Tangle (1965)
Maid in Paris (1966)
Margin for Terror (1967)

NON-SERIES
Liz (1955)
Key Witness (1956)
The Living End (1957)
Syndicate Girl (1958)
Juke Box King (1959)
The Line-Up (TV tie-in, 1959)
The Conspirators (1962)

AS BY FRANK BOYD
The Flesh Peddlers (1959)
Johnny Stacccato (TV tie-in;1960)

NON-FICTION
Anatomy of the Whiskey Business (1965)
Travel is for the Birds (1966; travel)
Louis S. Rosenstiel: Industry Statesman (2 vols,
  1966)

Frank Kane was born in Brooklyn on July 19, 1912. Graduating from New York City College at 19, he began to attend law school when the first of three daughters were born to him and his wife, Ann. Needing the extra income, he began to work as a newspaper columnist, working his way up to editor before becoming a public relations director for the liquor indus-try. After WWII, Kane left public relations to become a freelance writer and a radio and TV producer. He wrote for *The Shadow* for six years, but it was the creation of detective Johnny Liddell in *About Face* which made his fortune. Selling millions of copies throughout the world, Kane eventually wrote nearly 40 novels, most of them Liddell mysteries, and ended up working in Hollywood where he created his own production company. He passed away unexpectedly at his home in Manhasset, New York, on November 29, 1968.

Black Gat Books

Black Gat Books is a new line of mass market paperbacks introduced in 2015 by Stark House Press. New titles appear every three months, featuring the best in crime fiction reprints. Each book is sized to 4.25" x 7", just like they used to be. Collect them all! $9.99 each.

1 Haven for the Damned
by Harry Whittington
978-1-933586-75-5

2 Eddie's World
by Charlie Stella
978-1-933586-76-2

3 Stranger at Home
by Leigh Brackett writing as George Sanders
978-1-933586-78-6

4 The Persian Cat
by John Flagg
978-1933586-90-8

5 Only the Wicked
by Gary Phillips
978-1-933586-93-9

6 Felony Tank
by Malcolm Braly
978-1-933586-91-5

7 The Girl on the Bestseller List
by Vin Packer
978-1-933586-98-4

8 She Got What She Wanted
by Orrie Hitt
978-1-944520-04-5

9 The Woman on he Roof
by Helen Nielsen
978-1-944520-13-7

10 Angel's Flight
by Lou Cameron
978-1-944520-18-2

11 The Affair of Lady Westcott's Lost Ruby / The Case of the Unseen Assassin
by Gary Lovisi
978-1-944520-22-9

12 The Last Notch
by Arnold Hano
978-1-944520-31-1

13 Never Say No to a Killer
by Clifton Adams
978-1-944520-36-6

14 The Men from the Boys
by Ed Lacy
978-1-944520-46-5

15 Frenzy of Evil
by Henry Kane
978-1-944520-53-3

16 You'll Get Yours
by William Ard
978-1-944520-54-0

17 End of the Line
by Dolores & Bert Hitchens
978-1-944520-57-1

18 Frantic
by Noël Calef
978-1-944520-66-3

19 The Hoods Take Over
by Ovid Demaris
978-10944520-73-1

20 Madball by Fredric Brown
978-1-944520-74-8

21 Stool Pigeon
by Louis Malley
978-1-944520-81-6

Stark House Press

1315 H Street, Eureka, CA 95501 707-498-3135
griffinskye3@sbcglobal.net www.starkhousepress.com

Available from your local bookstore or direct from the publisher.